WEDDING GAMES

EVIE ALEXANDER

EMLIN
PRESS

First Published in Great Britain 2023 by Emlin Press

ISBN (eBook) 978-1-914473-18-0

ISBN (Print) 978-1-914473-19-7

A CIP catalogue record for this book is available from the British Library.

www.emlinpress.com

EMLIN
PRESS

To my husband

Cupid Calamity

Cookout Carnage

Christmas Chaos

Find all Evie's books at

www.eviealexanderauthor.com

EMLIN
PRESS

PROLOGUE

I t is a truth universally acknowledged, that a single man in possession of a good fortune must be in want of a wife. This particular single man, with his impressively large fortune, had found his perfect candidate and was about to marry her in Inverness cathedral.

The wedding was deemed so important by the elite and those who liked to read about them, that a minor European royal postponed his own nuptials to the following weekend rather than have half his celebrity friends fail to appear. And an invitation was so coveted that one lucky recipient ran a charity auction for the opportunity to be their plus one.

Other guests simply accepted bribes.

The moment the engagement was announced, a bidding war for the media rights began. The winning company, keen to protect its investment, paid for Typhoon jets from RAF Lossiemouth to patrol the airspace above the wedding. To cover the ground, they seconded the Royal Highland Fusiliers, 2nd Battalion. If that wasn't enough, all guests were searched and scanned on arrival at each location, and had agreed that 'if clarification was required', they would submit to a body cavity examination.

Standing at the altar in a tailor-made kilt, the roar of the aircraft rattling the stained-glass windows, Rory MacGinley, the Earl of Kinloch, wondered for the umpteenth time that day if any of it was really necessary. He'd wanted this wedding to be as quiet and low-key as possible. However, there was a cast of thousands, more foliage than an Amsterdam flower market, and despite a ban on secular music in God's house, he was convinced the thirty bagpipers had been playing Whitney Houston's *I Will Always Love You* as he'd proceeded up the aisle a few minutes earlier.

'Who gives this woman to be married to this man?' the minister asked loudly.

This was it. The moment he could never have imagined in a thousand lifetimes. One so surreal, he still expected to wake and find it had all been a very bad dream.

He cleared his throat. 'I do.'

His mother smiled at him, radiant with happiness. He gritted his teeth in return and reluctantly released her hand to the man standing before them—Brad Bauer.

Multi-millionaire, megastar, and twelve years his fiancée's junior, Brad was the last person in the galaxy Rory wanted to marry his mother. More plastic than a Ken doll, more ostentatious than a peacock at a drag competition, and more enthusiastic than a cheerleading squad at the Super Bowl, Brad was the polar opposite to Rory in every single way.

However, his mother, Barbara, had made her decision and there was nothing he could do about it. The only positives were that Brad seemed genuine in his devotion, and after the wedding, the happy couple were buggering off to live in LA.

They would be out of sight, out of mind, and Rory would be left in peace with the love of his life.

As the minister continued with the ceremony, he sat next to Zoe in the front pew with a sigh, interlacing his calloused fingers with hers. She squeezed his hand to reassure him and rested her head on his shoulder. Despite his harsh upbringing, the challenges of managing an estate and crumbling castle, and this latest curveball thrown by Brad, Rory considered himself the luckiest man alive. Zoe Maxwell was the fire that kept his life burning and she'd agreed to be his wife. He wanted them married as soon as possible, but they had to get this wedding out of the way first.

Zoe squeezed his hand tighter and he glanced up. He'd been successfully tuning out the ceremony, but it seemed things were going a little off script.

'Babe,' Brad gushed to Barbara, tears flowing down his tanned cheeks. 'I'm gonna worship and adore you. I swear, baby. The Bradster's gonna obey the f—fudge outta you. 'Cos you're my queen, and I'm your servant for, like, eternal life.' Brad turned to the crowd behind him. 'Eternal life!' he yelled.

Half the congregation whooped, and everyone who was British, flinched.

Brad returned his attention to his bride, gazing at her as if she'd created a new universe where war, hunger, and injustice no longer existed, and unicorns farted rainbows.

'This heart—' He punched his chest. 'Beats only for you.'

Rory sank lower in his seat.

'This brain—' Brad smacked his forehead. 'Works only for you.'

Please stop talking.

'This body—'

Oh god, no.

Brad flexed his arms and jerked his hips forward. 'Fu—'

3

'Bradley!' Barbara hissed, cutting him off.

'Yes, Countess?'

Barbara's expression softened as she cupped his face and wiped his tears with her thumbs.

'It's okay,' she said quietly. 'I know.'

Two months later

Zoe's mother, Mary, dabbed at her eyes with a handkerchief.

'My darling wee girl, you're a picture.'

Mary reached for a champagne flute with her free hand and took a large glug, as if hoping additional alcohol would dampen, not amplify the emotional fires set off by wedding dress shopping with her only child.

'Mum, when have I ever been "wee"?'

Standing at just over five foot ten, with a mop of curly red hair that added at least a couple of inches to her height, Zoe Maxwell had never felt small. That was until she met and fell in love with Rory. Her fiancé was fifty per cent mountain, fifty per cent bear, and one hundred per cent man. Next to him she felt tiny and treasured as well as strong and sexy. With Rory, she felt everything.

Staring at her reflection in the full-length mirror, dressed in an ivory silk gown, she felt a thrill race through her as she remembered the first time they'd ever kissed. She'd been wearing her friend Fiona's wedding dress as Fiona took pictures of her and Rory for the Kinloch estate website. The aim was to show people what their photos might look like if they chose the castle for their wedding. Everything about the shoot had been respectable. Until the moment Fiona left them alone in a room with a four-poster bed...

'Are you alright, Miss Maxwell? Is it too tight?'

Zoe fanned her flaming cheeks, trying to waft away the memories that were seared into her soul like a brand. She smiled at the boutique owner. 'I'm fine, but I'd love to try on another one if possible?'

'Of course.' The woman rushed to a large rack at the side of the private changing room. The bridal boutique was opulent, with thick carpets and velvet sofas. It was designed to make any woman feel like royalty, but Zoe could still see the disbelief in the owner's eyes that the future Countess of Kinloch was buying a dress off the peg. 'We've just had a new delivery of some exclusive designer numbers from Edinburgh,' she said. 'With your figure, they'll be absolutely stunning.'

'She looks like a model in everything,' added her mother.

'That she does,' the woman agreed. 'Whatever she chooses, it won't need any alteration.'

As Zoe slipped into another frock, Mary reached for her handkerchief again.

'A perfect dress for a perfect day,' she sighed.

Zoe smiled. Both she and Rory weren't fussed about having a big wedding. For them, it wasn't about the event, it was about the result. Rory would have preferred they were married an hour after she accepted his proposal.

But with her parents in London, his mother and step-father in LA, and their friends living around the globe, twenty minutes in a registry office followed by a pub lunch wasn't going to cut it. And now that she was trying on these magical dresses, she also had to admit she wanted to feel like a princess for a day.

'Aye, that's the one,' exclaimed her mother.

'You've said that about every dress,' Zoe replied.

'Och, maybe I have, but they're all so bonny.'

Zoe gave her mother a look. Mary was born in Kinloch and lived there until her late twenties. After leaving for London, she'd only returned to Scotland three times, and Zoe couldn't remember her ever using words like 'aye', 'wee', 'och', or 'bonny'. But since that morning, when she'd flown up to help Zoe choose a dress, she was sounding increasingly Scottish by the minute.

After their appointment at the boutique, they were going to see Morag, Mary's childhood friend, and spend the rest of the day and evening with her before Mary returned to London the following morning. Her mother hadn't seen Morag for years. Being back in the Highlands and about to reconnect with her old friend, her accent was also finding its way home.

'Which dress do you prefer, love?' her mum asked.

Zoe swished the long skirts. A panel, in tartan, ran from the bodice down to the bottom hem.

'Would you be able to replace the panel with the MacGinley colours?' she asked the owner.

'Of course. We can have it ready in a week if that works for you?'

'Yes, thank you. And does this dress have one of those hidden buttons so I can dance in it?'

The woman lifted the hem and showed Zoe how to shorten it. 'Here you go. Now the earl can whirl you around the floor without any accidents.'

Zoe grinned. 'Sold. I love it.'

Her mother, normally the most down-to-earth woman Zoe

knew, squealed like a tween at her first pop concert, then necked the rest of the champagne.

'Zoe, ma darling, you're going to be the most beautiful bride in the whole wide world.'

TWO HOURS LATER, ZOE STEPPED OUT OF THE BACK DOOR OF Morag's house for some much needed quiet. One summer, as a child, she'd stayed with her great uncle Willie in the cabin where she now lived with Rory. At the time, Morag had been a second mum to her and she'd spent her days running wild with Morag's children, Fiona and Jamie. As an adult, she became closer to the family, the bond strengthening even further when Jamie began to date her best friend, Sam. Family meals at Morag's were always loud, but with her mother and Morag drunkenly reminiscing about their youth, Zoe's eardrums needed a break.

She leaned against the stone wall and closed her eyes, letting the August sun warm her face and the solid stone muffle the shrieks of laughter from inside. The past ten months had been nuts. She'd moved to a different country, fallen in love with a man who turned out to be an earl, seen a Hollywood blockbuster filmed at his castle, and watched the biggest movie star on the planet marry her future mother-in-law. And on top of all that, Zoe was a month shy of becoming the Countess of Kinloch.

'Zoe?'

She jumped. 'Oh my god, Rory, you scared the shit out of me! Where did you come from?'

He looked confused. 'I've been calling your name as I walked up. Why are you shouting?'

'I'm not shouting.'

He winced.

'Am I?'

He nodded. 'I take it Morag's operating at top volume?'

'Yep. I think I'd rather stand next to your chainsaw without ear-defenders for an hour than go back in.'

He looked sceptical. 'But your mum's fairly chill, isn't she?'

On cue, a scream of laughter from inside cut through the kitchen windows.

'My mum has either snorted a kilo of cocaine or had her personality genetically amplified,' Zoe replied. 'You remember my mum, right? Sings in the church choir? Works in a charity shop?'

Rory grinned.

'Well,' Zoe continued. 'That, in there,' she gestured to the house, 'is a banshee crossed with a hellion. Did you get what I asked you for?'

He held up a bottle of Prosecco.

'No, no, Jesus Christ, no. They've had more than enough already.'

He burst out laughing. 'Since when did you ever hold back on drinking Prosecco?'

Zoe drew a breath, preparing to shoot his accusation down in flames, but realised she couldn't contradict him, so she stuck her tongue out.

Rory raised his eyebrow in response and took a small box from the pocket of his shirt.

'Is this what you need?' he mouthed.

'Ha-de-ha,' she replied, taking it. She pulled out two sets of foam ear plugs and handed him a pair. 'In five minutes you'll thank me, I promise.'

'Rory!' screeched Zoe's mum, leaping to her feet. She didn't appear to notice the dining chair clattering to the floor behind her as she lurched towards him with the haste of a peri-menopausal woman with a hot flush spying a walk-in fridge.

'Ma favourite future son-in-law!'

Rory leaned down into her embrace. 'Hey, Mary, how was your flight up?'

'Och, you were so kind to buy it for me. I tell you though, it was up and down faster than a nun's knickers. Ooh, and I had some salty nuts.'

'Mum!'

'Said the actress to the bishop,' cackled Morag.

The two older women howled with laughter as Zoe caught Rory's eye. He pointed to his ear and mouthed 'thank you', then glanced around the room with a look of alarm.

Zoe knew he'd been expecting other people at dinner. Morag's boyfriend, Big Jim, was meant to be there, as well as Fiona and her husband, Duncan, with their son, Liam. Their presence was meant to dilute the combined effect of two women who had reached the age where they'd ceased to care what most people thought of them.

Mary steered Rory into a chair and Morag deposited a cote de boeuf steak on a plate in front of him.

'Tuck in, big man,' urged Morag. 'We've already eaten and you're looking a little pale.'

'Where's Fi, Dunc, and Liam?' he asked.

Morag rolled her eyes. 'They said it was too loud for the wee one and took him home.'

'And Jim?'

Morag looked off into the middle distance, a smile on her face. 'He didn't want to interrupt our girly catch up. He's so thoughtful.'

Rory cleared his throat. 'Indeed. And I think Zoe and I should get out of your hair as well.'

'No, no, no!' cried Mary.

'We don't want to cramp your style,' he continued.

Mary pulled his head to her chest and smothered him in a tight embrace. 'You're such a good man. How did you turn out so different from your father?'

'MUM!'

Mary leapt back, her hand over her mouth. 'Oops! Sorry, Rory.'

He smiled. 'It's okay, Mary. I know exactly what he was like. You don't have to pretend he was something different just because he's dead.'

'It's just you look so much like him,' Mary continued, staring at Rory with unfocussed eyes.

Zoe could see his shoulders start to hunch. The last thing he ever wanted was to be likened to his dad.

'Mum, Morag, why don't we go into the kitchen, and let Rory eat his steak in peace?'

'You have his looks but you don't have his personality,' said Mary, completely ignoring her daughter. She frowned. 'And it's not like you have your mum's, either.'

Oh god. If her mother was skating on thin ice talking about Rory's father, now she was about to smash it with a sledgehammer.

'Och, aye,' agreed Morag.

'Mum, Morag,' Zoe said sharply. 'Kitchen.'

Mary patted Rory's head as if he was the faithful family dog.

'You're so kind. And caring. And thoughtful. But your mum—'

A loud banging on the back door stopped Mary before Zoe did.

Thank fuck.

Morag glanced at her watch. 'I wonder who that could be,'

she mumbled, before giving an exaggerated wink to Mary. 'I wonder if it's Big Jim wanting a booty call.'

Mary snorted with laughter and Zoe grabbed her arm as Morag left the room.

'Sit down,' she hissed in her mother's ear. 'And don't say another word about Rory's parents.'

Her mum nodded and pantomimed zipping her mouth shut.

With the ear plugs in, Zoe couldn't hear Morag's exchange in the kitchen. She glanced across the dining room table at Rory, who shrugged. He cut a big piece off his steak and started eating.

Morag opened the door, her face cycling through twenty different expressions, none of them positive.

Behind her, entering the room with a look of disdain reserved for a toddler who just crapped in her swimming pool, was Lady Barbara Bauer, the Dowager Countess of Kinloch.

Rory started choking.

Zoe leapt to her feet but Barbara got to him first. She whacked him between the shoulder blades with enough force to jerk his upper body forward. A chunk of meat flew out of his mouth and knocked over an unfinished bottle of Prosecco. It crashed into a glass on its way down, smashing it to pieces.

Rory was on his feet. 'I'll do the glass.'

'Lordy!' said Morag, throwing napkins onto the table as if expecting them to become sentient and start mopping up the mess.

Rory carefully picked up the pieces of glass as Zoe and Mary cleared the rest of the dishes.

Barbara simply watched. Her lips a thin line, her back ramrod straight.

Zoe snuck glances at Rory. His mum was meant to be in

LA. What the fuck was she doing here? Rory's jaw was set with tension and he didn't return her gaze.

All too soon the table was cleared and silence fell thick around them.

'Barbara,' said Morag, brightly. 'What a pleasant and unexpected surprise. Can I offer you a drink?'

Barbara shook her head, her focus solely on Rory.

'No, thank you. I'm here for my son.'

'Is everything okay?' Zoe asked, remembering Barbara's cancer scare earlier in the year.

Barbara frowned at her. 'Why are you shouting?'

'Mum, what's happened? I thought you were in LA.'

Barbara's jerked her head back. 'And why are *you* shouting? I'm not deaf. Stop bellowing like a half-wit.'

Rory and Zoe removed their ear plugs.

'Eh?' said Morag, loudly. 'Why are you wearing them?'

Barbara looked at Morag and raised a perfect eyebrow as if transferring the half-wit status to her.

Rory and Zoe blushed.

'I'm here to see if my only child is alive,' said Barbara, addressing Rory. 'Seeing as how he's been ignoring my emails and phone calls for the past two weeks.'

Zoe looked at him. 'Rory?'

'And I haven't been able to reach *you*,' Barbara continued, now eyeballing Zoe, 'because you've never given me any of your contact details.'

'I wonder why,' Mary muttered.

Zoe held her breath as Barbara's head swivelled to face her mum.

'Mrs Maxwell,' she enunciated. 'Despite the ravages of Father Time, I see some things haven't changed.'

'Mum!' snapped Rory. 'Let's discuss this at the castle.'

Morag grabbed Mary's arm and pulled her to the door. 'No need. We'll give you a bit of space.'

Zoe dithered. Should she clear off, or did Rory need her support?

'Please stay, dear,' said Barbara. 'This concerns you as well.'

The door shut and Zoe sat next to Rory. Barbara positioned herself across the table from them, her hands steepled as if about to fire them both for misconduct.

They waited until they could hear the sounds of the television from the living room next door, then Zoe spoke.

'Rory, what is going on, and why have you been ignoring your mum?'

Barbara inclined her head as if giving the floor to him.

He cleared his throat.

'I'm sorry. To you, Mum, for not having a much needed conversation, and to you, Zoe for not telling you about it.'

'About what?' she asked, anxiety pricking at her stomach.

'The wedding.'

'The wedding?' she squeaked, her heart in her mouth. 'Are you calling it off?'

'Oh god, no! Fuck no! Not at all! No!'

'What is it then?' she asked, her heart hammering.

'It's the guest list, the press, the stuff we haven't planned.'

'I don't understand.'

Barbara sighed. 'Zoe. I appreciate you feel this wedding should be your day, however, when you marry the Earl of Kinloch there are certain expectations.'

'There are? Like what?'

'This is a society wedding, and as such, society must be invited.'

'What kind of society?'

Rory reached for her hand. 'We don't have to do any of this.'

His mother ignored him, focusing her attention on Zoe.

'The right kind, not gossip rag fodder who turn up to the opening of an envelope. You may not be aware, but my late husband had an extended family, and it is expected, as well as courteous, to invite them. The Foxbrookes, for example. Well, the legitimate ones at least.'

'But I don't know them. This is my—our wedding.' She looked at Rory. 'Do you want them there?'

He rubbed his thumb across the back of her hand. 'You know what I think. I don't care if it's us and your—our parents.' He looked at his mother. 'All of this is irrelevant. We can't afford it.'

Barbara took a breath.

'No,' Rory said, cutting her off.

His mother pressed her lips together as if steeling herself to remain in control then took a measured breath.

'I was going to suggest a compromise.'

'Compromise?' Zoe and Rory uttered in unison.

Barbara blinked. 'Up until this year, my entire life has been a compromise,' she replied, icily.

'Sorry,' said Zoe, automatically. Barbara was right. She'd had a difficult childhood, and the apparent victory at marrying Rory's father at the age of eighteen had come at a huge personal cost.

'I am suggesting you invite whoever you want to a few days of festivities leading up to the main event,' Barbara began. 'Bradley has been enlightening me as to the American custom of holding a "rehearsal dinner", which would be an excellent way of having the kind of intimate celebration you seek. I understand the financial concerns when you still have an estate to manage, so my husband and I are offering to foot the bill for the entire wedding.' She paused. 'In exchange for being able to add extra attendees to the wedding day itself.'

'No,' replied Rory.

'How many?' asked Zoe, squeezing his hand. Even though they'd planned a small celebration, she would rather the money was put into the estate.

'Five hundred,' Barbara replied.

'Oh my god!'

'No, no, no,' said Rory. 'That's nuts.'

Barbara sighed. 'Is it? Take the Foxbrookes. If you include the illegitimates, that's ten people. And if any of the children are wed, that number only increases.'

'No,' Rory repeated.

Zoe elbowed him. 'One hundred and fifty,' she said to Barbara.

'Four hundred,' she replied, her cornflower blue eyes glinting with victory. 'And exclusive rights given to Vanity Fair or Vogue.'

'Zoe—'

'Two hundred,' said Zoe, cutting him off. 'We have a veto on all pictures and the fee goes to a charity of our choice.'

'Three hundred and fifty, and the gift list is with Harrods.'

'Two hundred and twenty-five. No gift list but charity donations encouraged.'

'Three hundred. And your dress is couture.'

'No. I've already bought it. Two hundred and fifty, and whoever the Foxbrooke illegitimates are, they still get an invite.'

Barbara raised an eyebrow. 'Two hundred and seventy-five. That's my final offer.'

'Two hundred and fifty is mine.'

Silence.

'Deal,' said Barbara, extending her hand.

Zoe shook it.

Rory sighed and hung his head.

$$\text{\s}\quad 2 \quad \text{\s}$$

Tuesday – Four days before the wedding

In his adult life, Rory had been dumped from a great height by his ex-fiancée, been thrown out of aeroplanes, been shot at too many times to count, and survived being blown up. However, none of these gut-churning situations created the same sort of anxiety as the prospect of spending an evening watching his mother and future mother-in-law circle each other like stags spoiling for a fight.

Zoe's mother and his parents had grown up in Kinloch but were each separated by a decade. Mary was ten years older than Barbara, his mum, and Rory's father had been ten years older still. His dad had been a playboy, but had decided to settle down upon turning forty. His eye landed on Zoe's mum, but when she refused him, he decided 'no' was a word he no longer understood or accepted. Barbara, only just turned eighteen and fiercely ambitious, had set her heart on the title of Countess and saw Mary as an obstacle to be removed.

The situation got completely out of hand and was only

resolved when Zoe's mum ran away to England with Zoe's dad, and his father paid proper attention to the beautiful teenager trying to catch his eye.

Now Barbara and Mary were meeting formally again.

Zoe had suggested a dinner on neutral territory at a restaurant in Inverness. However, with Brad being one of the most recognisable faces on the planet, interference from the public would not have helped with social bonding. Rory didn't want them to use the cabin for the meal. It was too small to contain such big personalities, and he wanted to be able to escape to it if everything went south.

The castle was the compromise. Rather than use the long, rectangular table in the dining room, a round one was set up in the library, so no person was perceived to have a preferential position at it. Barbara and Mary were to be placed on either side of Rory, with Brad and Arnold on either side of Zoe. Clive, the owner of Kinloch's only pub, had been drafted in for the night with his daughter, Kayleigh. Other waiting staff were assisting, with one of Clive's chefs in charge of the food.

Rory hoped that Clive's presence in the room would help curb his mother's tongue, but he was leaving nothing to chance. The lighting was flatteringly low and designed to cover micro-expressions of animosity, the food had been selected to please everyone's palates, and Zoe had hidden aromatherapy diffusers around the room filled with relaxing essential oils. The meeting had been planned with more care and redundancies built in than one between rival Afghan warlords.

That morning, Mary and Arnold had completed their drive up from England and were resting at Morag's house, where they were staying for the week of the wedding. Barbara and Brad had flown in from LA by private jet and were staying in the castle's self-contained flat.

At six fifty-eight p.m., his stomach in knots, Rory stood by the front door, awaiting Zoe who was bringing her parents.

At six fifty-nine p.m., his mother glided down the main staircase, Brad on her arm. They made a blindingly beautiful couple. Barbara was bedecked in jewels and wearing the same gown she wore to celebrate her first engagement nearly thirty-five years ago. Brad was in full Highland dress with a sporran big enough to hold a family-sized haggis.

At seven p.m., there was a knock at the door.

Rory opened it. 'Mary—'

'Welcome to Kinloch castle,' his mother interrupted, pushing him out of the way. 'On behalf of my husband and I, allow me to formally welcome you to the nuptial celebrations of the Earl of Kinloch.'

Barbara ignored Mary, extending her hand to Arnold. He took it, mouth open, seemingly flummoxed by the welcome.

'How delightful,' said Mary, loudly. 'And which incredible woman is the extremely lucky earl marrying?'

'This one!' whooped Brad, grabbing Zoe and lifting her off the ground. 'Congrats, babe!' He set her down and grasped Mary's shoulders. 'I can sure see where Zoe gets her beauty from.' He kissed her cheeks. 'I'm Brad,' he announced, before turning to Arnold and pumping his hand. 'You must be Arnold. Great to meet you, man.'

Arnold and Mary stared at him, finally face-to-face with the Hollywood legend.

Rory caught Zoe's eye. She looked as nervous as he felt.

'You're so handsome,' stated Arnold.

Brad attempted to look coy as he soaked up the adoration.

'And your teeth are so white,' Arnold continued. 'How? Do you have a special toothpaste?'

'Dad!' Zoe hissed.

Brad leaned closer. 'Veneers, man.'

Arnold looked confused. 'What, like wood?'

Brad laughed and clapped him on the back. 'I like you.'

'Shall we move to the library?' Rory asked, not waiting for a reply as he gripped his mother's arm and frogmarched her along the corridor.

'For the love of god, will you behave?' he spat through gritted teeth.

'I'm trying,' she hissed.

'You certainly are,' he replied, his voice laden with sarcasm. 'Look, I don't care if you never speak to them again after the wedding, but please, be civil for the next few days.'

His mum nodded her head and the knot in his stomach loosened slightly. Now he had to hope Mary didn't rise to any more of his mother's baiting.

They entered the library and took their seats.

'Mary, Arnold,' Rory began, keen to steer the conversation. 'It's lovely to see you again. How was the drive up?'

'Not bad,' Arnold replied. 'Just so much longer than expected. We set off yesterday and it took almost an hour to get to the M25. Can you believe it? Every car on the road was a lorry. We settled on the M1 up to Rugby, averaging sixty miles per hour due to the roadworks, and stopped at Toddington services to stretch our legs and avail ourselves of the facilities.'

As Arnold talked, Clive moved around the table serving drinks.

'You know,' Arnold continued, 'I still can't get over how many choices of coffee there are at these places. There was a Costa at Toddington. I had an Americano and Mary had a Latte. They did a lovely pattern in the foam on the top for her. Terribly clever stuff. At Rugby, we joined the M6, then took the M42 around Birmingham, and splashed out by taking the M6 toll to save a bit of time. But once we were back on the M6 proper, it was just more roadworks.'

'Sounds tough,' said Brad. 'Why didn't you fly?'

There was an awkward pause. Zoe's parents didn't have much money, and even though he and Zoe wanted to pay for their tickets as they'd done for Mary a month ago, this time Zoe's parents refused.

'We had so much luggage,' replied Mary. 'It made sense to take the car. And it gave us a chance to break our journey in the Lake District.'

'Well, next time, borrow my plane,' said Brad with a smile.

'Oh my goodness, we couldn't possibly,' replied Mary.

Brad shrugged. 'Sure you can. I've got one just for the UK. The pilots and crew don't like to be bored.'

'But—'

'You're family now,' said Brad. He thumped the centre of his chest as if to emphasise the point. 'Family.'

'Clive,' said Rory, trying to move the meal on. 'Are you ready to serve the first course?'

Clive nodded and snapped his fingers at his daughter who scurried out of the room.

'Ladies and gentlemen,' he began. 'Our first course is a mezze platter of food from the estate. We have smoked salmon, Aberdeen Angus bresaola, wild boar prosciutto, and smoked wild duck. In addition, we have a selection of salad leaves grown at the Kinloch community farm and griddled halloumi from the Clun Forest flock. There are also freshly baked flatbreads served with cultured butter.'

Rory glanced around the table at the smiles. At least the food would hit the spot, even if the company was at odds.

'So, Mary,' Brad said. 'You grew up in Kinloch?'

Mary nodded.

'Do you know Morag? Doll that runs the post office?'

She smiled broadly. 'We've been friends since before either of us can remember.'

'Hot damn!' Brad whistled. 'Tell me more.'

Mary blushed. 'We were rather naughty growing up. Well, as naughty as you can be in a small village with nothing much to do and extremely strict parents.'

Kayleigh re-appeared and put platters on the table so they could help themselves.

'In those days,' Mary continued, 'we had to make our own fun. The internet didn't exist and my mother didn't have a television. She believed it corrupted the mind.'

Brad laughed. 'What do you think she would have made of one of my films?'

Mary grimaced. 'I'm afraid she would have consigned you to a fiery pit in hell. She was a bit of a dragon.'

Brad looked pleased with this response. 'Any siblings?'

She shook her head. 'Only me.'

Brad turned to Barbara. 'And did you join in? Were you a naughty girl too?' he asked, wiggling his eyebrows.

Rory held his breath.

His mother's face was impassive. 'I wasn't yet born when they were caught stealing apples from the estate. Although—' Her unlined brow furrowed slightly. 'I believe I was seven when they graduated to cider making.' Her expression turned sourer than month-old milk. 'The bottles exploded as they were carrying them at night down the high street, and the corks broke two windows.'

Brad hooted with laughter. 'I like your style, Mary. Arnold, are you from Scotland? How did you two meet?'

Arnold placed a hand over his heart. 'It was a love story to rival one of your films.'

Brad's eyes gleamed as if beholding dollar signs humping Oscar statuettes. 'Go on,' he urged, leaning forward.

Mary and Zoe reached for their glasses of wine. Despite many years as a teetotaller, Rory wondered if now might be the time to start drinking alcohol again. Arnold's monologues could make a raver on amphetamines nod off.

Arnold sat back in his chair, cracking his neck before speaking. 'Well, I may resemble a handsome city slicker—'

Barbara coughed into her wine glass.

'—but underneath this polished exterior lurks a rugged man of the mountains.'

Barbara snorted.

Rory kicked his mother's foot under the table as Mary glared daggers across the table at her.

'I'd always been fascinated by the Aborigine custom of walkabout,' Arnold continued. 'Just you and the wilderness. A spiritual journey and rite of passage. Man versus wild. But the only place in the UK I could find the solitude for this kind of challenge was in the Highlands. So, I saved up my annual leave and all my pennies and took the train north.'

'Love it,' said Brad decisively. He held a hand up to Arnold as if to pause his speech and leaned back in his chair to look at Clive. 'Dude, you got a spare napkin and pen?'

Clive took a waiter's pad out of his top pocket and handed it to Brad along with a biro.

'Thanks, man.' Brad scribbled a few notes and then looked at Arnold. 'Continue.'

Arnold seemed to inflate a little more and Rory braced himself. He'd already heard this story several times and, like an angler describing the size of fish they'd caught, Arnold's story got bigger and more dramatic with each re-telling.

'I strode into the wilderness armed only with a few meagre supplies, my Swiss Army penknife, and my battered copy of *Scouting for Boys*.'

Brad whistled. 'I'm getting *Deliverance* and *The Revenant* vibes already.'

'It was the height of summer, and I was a sitting duck for the worst predators Scotland has ever known.'

'Snakes?' Brad asked, excitedly.

Arnold shook his head.

'Wolves?'

'Far worse. These attack day and night with no mercy,' Arnold replied.

'Holy cow. Goblins?'

'Bradley,' said Barbara. 'We've already had this conversation.'

'These beasts can drain a man in under an hour,' said Arnold, solemnly.

Rory shut his eyes briefly, wishing the whole evening to be over when he opened them again.

'Frikking vampires!' Brad yelled, standing up and punching the air. 'Knew it!'

'Bradley!' Barbara hissed. 'Sit!'

As he sat, Mary giggled into her wine glass.

Barbara shot her a venomous look.

Arnold shook his head. 'If only. I could have dealt with them easily as I was carrying a spare wooden stake and an emergency vial of holy water.'

'Skills,' murmured Brad, nodding his head.

'The beasts that were after my blood,' continued Arnold, pausing for dramatic effect, 'were midges.'

Brad's face blanched. 'You weren't wearing any Avon *Skin So Soft*?'

Arnold shook his head. 'I was untried and untested. And the mistake proved almost fatal.'

'So, what did you do?'

'I found a bog and covered myself in mud.'

'Like Rambo!'

Arnold nodded. 'It saved my skin and disguised my scent, enabling me to hunt for food.'

Rory could see Mary's lips pressed tight together. She was not going to undermine her husband's story in front of Barbara, even though she'd gleefully torn his tall tale to pieces when Rory had first heard it.

'Speaking of food,' Rory said. 'Clive, I think we're ready for the next course?'

Clive nodded and left the room as Kayleigh cleared their plates.

'What did you hunt?' Brad asked.

'Grouse, pheasant and rabbits mainly. I also wrestled a deer, but it got away.'

Clive re-entered the room with extra waiters carrying plates.

'Pan seared venison loin with a wild bilberry sauce, roast potatoes in goose fat, and summer greens from the community garden,' he announced with a flourish as they were presented with their food.

Rory only ate meat, so he had the venison with a side order of fatty beef ribs. He ate quickly, shovelling food in, hoping that everyone else followed his lead and the meal could be over in the next ten minutes.

'This is delicious,' said Mary. 'Rory, did you shoot it?'

'Or wrestle it?' Barbara added.

He ignored his mother's jibe. 'Not this one, Mary, but it is from here.'

Mary nodded. 'How are the last-minute preparations going for the big day?'

'Great,' said Zoe. 'Sam and Jamie and Charlie and Valentina arrive tomorrow. We're going to do the final fitting for the bridesmaid's dresses before the rehearsal dinner.'

'Well, darling, just let me know if there's anything I can do to help,' Mary replied. 'I want to make sure your special day is perfect.'

'Thank you for your offer,' Barbara said. 'But it is entirely unnecessary. We have everything in hand.' She turned to Rory, not allowing Mary to reply. 'You still haven't answered my question about your decisions for decorating the flat in the castle. I'm sure you wish to put your stamp on it before you move in?'

Rory opened his mouth to speak.

'We're going to keep on living in the cabin,' said Zoe.

Barbara lowered her cutlery, her eyes wide. 'You can't possibly be serious?'

'Why not?' asked Mary.

Barbara kept her gaze fixed on her future daughter-in-law. 'The Earl and Countess of Kinloch residing in a one-room labourer's cabin? When this?'—she gestured around her—'is available and more appropriately befits your status?'

'Whatever will the neighbours think?' Mary added with a sarcastic gasp.

Rory's heart rate spiked.

Zoe shot her mother a look across the table. 'We are very happy in the cabin, Barbara, and can manage the estate without living on-site.'

'But what about children? Are you going to be bringing them up there too? In vermin-infested mediaeval squalor?'

'We haven't yet discussed the matter,' Zoe continued.

'You haven't discussed children? But the family line!'

Rory cleared his throat. 'Mum. Zoe and I love the cabin and are very happy there. We appreciate there may come a time to move back to the castle, but that time is not now.'

Mary nodded. 'I understand how you feel. The cabin is so full of homely charm. Whereas the castle is rather cold and off-putting.'

Fuck's sake!

'Well—' Barbara began.

'Arnold!' exclaimed Brad. 'You didn't finish your story! Where does your grand romance with Mary come in?'

'Yes,' added Rory quickly. 'I don't think I've ever heard the full tale.'

Arnold was looking between Mary and Barbara as if watching an unstable nuclear reactor about to go critical. He smiled broadly, but it didn't reach his eyes.

'It was the hottest summer Scotland had seen for years, and the streams were dry. I was reduced to digging for water and eating my prey raw, but it wasn't enough.'

Arnold paused. Brad's hand was a blur as he made notes in shorthand on the pad Clive had given him.

'I became weak and delirious.'

'Yeah!' Brad exhaled.

'I saw visions.'

Brad took a sharp intake of breath. 'Silkies? Wulvers?' His pen trembled in his hand. 'The Black Dog?'

Arnold shook his head. 'I wish. These were worse.' He took a big mouthful of venison, chewing happily as Brad waited. 'My visions were of,' Arnold swallowed, 'food.'

'Food?'

'Mainly puddings. One moment a trifle would be sitting on a clump of heather, the next, poof! It was gone. It was torture. My lowest moment was when a spotted dick vanished as soon as I touched it.'

'Intense,' Brad breathed. 'What's a spotted dick?'

'It's a steamed pudding made with suet and currants,' Arnold replied. 'Absolutely delicious and best served with custard. I'll make you one if you want to try it?'

Brad reached across the table and high-fived him. 'Yeah, man! That would be sick!'

Rory signalled Clive to bring out the next course. Even though Brad and Arnold had not yet finished eating, Clive and his team cleared their plates and placed dessert in front of everyone bar Rory.

'Cranachan,' said Clive. 'With raspberries from the community garden.'

'Ooh!' said Arnold. 'It's like a trifle, but without the Lady Fingers.'

'Lady Fingers?' asked Brad.

'Sponge finger biscuits,' replied Arnold. 'You also use them in tiramisu.'

'Can you make me that as well?' asked Brad.

'Tiramisu? Or trifle?'

'Both?'

Arnold smiled. 'It would be my pleasure. A good pudding is what made me the man I am today.'

Barbara snorted and Mary took a big breath.

'Arnold!' Rory interrupted. 'You spotted Willie?'

'I thought it was Dick?' said Brad. 'Is Spotted Willy another pudding?'

Fuck my life. 'No,' Rory continued. 'Mary's uncle, Willie, found Arnold up on the glen and carried him back to Mary's mother's house. That's where Arnold met Mary.'

'Ror-eee,' complained Arnold. 'I was just getting to that bit!'

'Dad,' Zoe said, her spoon scraping the bottom of her bowl. 'Why don't you just give Brad the highlights now, then give him the director's cut another time?'

'Maybe I could take him up to the glen to see where I faced off against the adder?'

'Snakes!' yelled Brad happily as Mary and Barbara both shouted, 'no!' at the same time.

Arnold raised his hands as if to placate everyone. 'Okay,

okay, I'll give you the edited version of our sweeping love story.' He looked across the table at his wife, his expression soft. 'I finally passed out as Willie carried me off the glen. When I woke up, I was clean and warm, tucked up in a strange bed with an angel looking down at me. I remember blinking, thinking it must be a dream. But it wasn't. It was reality. I'd been through hell and entered paradise. I'd set off from London on an adventure to find myself, but instead, I found my soul.'

Mary's eyes welled up as she smiled at Arnold.

There was a loud sniff. 'That's beautiful, man. Frikking poetry.' Brad grabbed a napkin and blew his nose. 'And Mary? Had you ever met anyone like Arnold before?'

'No. I thought I would remain a spinster forever,' Mary replied. 'My mother was demanding and kept me at home. I didn't have any options and the single men in the village were completely unsuitable.'

Barbara sniffed.

'Too old, too ugly,' Mary continued. 'Or both.'

Barbara gasped.

Rory caught Zoe's eye across the table. The situation was deteriorating rapidly.

'Nobody was a suitable candidate. But then Arnold appeared like he was sent from heaven to rescue me. It was love at first sight, and before a week had passed, I packed a bag and ran away with him to England.' She sighed. 'It was meant to be.'

'Well—' Barbara began.

'Hot damn!' interjected Brad. 'We've got ourselves a movie!'

Rory pushed back his chair and stood, Zoe following his lead.

'I think this has been a great success,' he said.

'Did you want any coffee?' asked Clive.

'No thank you,' Zoe replied as she tugged her father's arm. 'I need to get these two back to Morag's. You alright with the clear up?'

'Yes, of course,' Clive replied, pulling Barbara's seat out so she could stand.

Brad was embracing Arnold. 'We need to get together again, man. This has been the bomb.'

'Absolutely!' Arnold replied. 'I should take you up to the glen.'

'No!' said Mary and Barbara again in unison.

Zoe marched her parents through the castle as if it was on fire, reaching the front door at least twenty yards ahead of Rory, his mother, and Brad.

'Thank you so much, see you tomorrow at the rehearsal dinner,' she called over her shoulder as she pushed them out into the courtyard.

Rory excused himself and followed her out. The September evening held a slight chill that was soothing to his skin.

Zoe ran back to him and he held her tightly in his arms.

'We survived,' she said into his chest.

'Only just.' He sighed. 'Fuck me, that was hard.'

'Yes please.'

'Huh?' He pulled back to look into her mischievous eyes.

She ground her hips into his and the penny dropped.

He grinned. 'Shall we leave your parents to Morag and go home?'

'Absolutely,' she replied. 'I want to see if your dick is spotted or not.'

＄ 3 ＆

Wednesday – Three days before the wedding

Inverness cathedral may have been a tourist attraction, but it was also a place of worship. The few people who'd been milling in the aisles peacefully admiring the architecture and communing with God were currently ducking for cover, their fingers in their ears, as the four horsewomen of the apocalypse reunited in front of the altar.

Sam, Zoe's best friend, was an actress and singer with the ability to project her voice into the next century. Small, blonde and bubbly, she was more effervescent than two litres of Coke meeting a packet of Mentos. Valentina was a Hollywood star, originally from Colombia, whose sparkling eyes, throaty laugh, and endless curves could make a statue come to life. Fiona was the only one of them with a child, but it was not slowing her down. She grabbed most social situations by the balls, cramming every second of fun in before heading home to relieve the babysitter.

Valentina had flown in late the previous night with Charlie,

Rory's best friend, and Sam had arrived at a similar time from London with Fiona's younger brother, Jamie. The four women hadn't had the opportunity to meet before the wedding rehearsal. Now they had their arms around each other in a circle, jumping and screaming as if they'd won the World Cup. Their other halves, Rory, Jamie, Charlie, and Duncan stood to one side as if denying all knowledge or association.

After the stress of the night before, Zoe was delirious with happiness. She had her people back. These three women didn't think she was too loud or too crazy. They loved and accepted her just the way she was, celebrated her light, and encouraged it to shine brighter. Right now, she felt like a supernova.

A wolf whistle loud enough to separate a dogfight finally got their attention. They turned to see Charlie, his fingers still in his mouth, and Rory pointing at the minister, who was looking shell-shocked.

'Ahem,' the minister began, eyes widening as he recognised Sam and Valentina. 'Shall we begin?'

AN HOUR LATER, THE REHEARSAL WAS OVER AND THE WOMEN were drinking champagne in the private changing room of the bridal boutique where Zoe had bought her wedding dress. Fiona had already been fitted for her bridesmaid's dress, and Sam and Valentina were trying theirs on. They had sent their measurements through a few weeks before.

The dresses were beautiful, with off the shoulder bodices and flowing gauze skirts. The colours were inspired by heather, with Sam in pale green, Fiona in deep purple, and Valentina in light purple. Individually, they were stunning, but together they were breathtaking.

Valentina was the first to notice Zoe's emotions.

'Chica!' she cried, squeezing her hand. 'Is everything okay? Are you unhappy with the dresses?'

Sam, who knew the difference between her best friend's happy and sad tears, lifted her skirt until the hem grazed her bottom.

'Yep, I feel you. Why on earth are we hiding these pins from the world? Can I grab a pair of scissors? Give my dress a bit of a prune?'

Zoe smiled through her tears as Fiona passed her a box of tissues.

'Honestly,' Sam continued. 'Valentina's in the gym like twenty-five hours a day. She shouldn't hide all that hard work. And Fi—'

'Is a mum who has never even seen the inside of a gym,' Fiona interrupted. 'Wait till Zoe and Rory have left the reception before you start lifting your skirts.'

'Oh, I won't be the one lifting them,' Sam replied. 'Once Jamie sees me in this, he'll drop to his knees, pull them up, and dive—'

'Shut-up, shut-up, shut-up!' screamed Fiona, slapping her hands to her ears. 'Eww! That's my *brother*!'

Zoe snorted with laughter.

'Sam and Jamie sitting in a tree,' sang Sam, 'F.U.C.K.I.N.G.'

'God, will you stop?' Fiona cried. 'I used to feel sorry for you, being saddled with my brother, but now I'm starting to feel sorry for *him*.'

Sam downed the last of her champagne and sang Tina Turner's 'Simply the Best' into the glass as if it were a microphone.

'Better than *what* rest?' Fiona scoffed. 'You're the only girl-friend he's ever had.'

Sam switched to Chesney Hawkes 'The One and Only',

holding a hairbrush out to Valentina. 'Come on, babe, I know you can sing.'

Valentina took it and they sang together, strutting around the room.

Fiona sank into a chair. Zoe passed her the bottle of champagne.

'Cheers, love.' Fiona didn't bother with a glass, pouring the fizz directly into her mouth as Sam and Valentina improvised a dance routine to go with the song.

Zoe's heart was full. Her wedding was one of those rare opportunities the four of them would be in the same place at the same time. She blinked, trying to record each moment as a snapshot in time to treasure later.

When Sam and Valentina finished their butchered rendition they bowed, and Zoe and Fiona clapped.

'What do you think, Zo?' asked Sam. 'Should we perform it at the wedding?'

'Jesus wept, no,' Fiona replied. 'I think the minister has had quite enough of us without adding that in.'

'I think you should have it up your sleeve in case of emergencies,' said Zoe. 'Like if my dad's speech goes over twenty minutes, or if Brad asks my mum to dance in front of Barbara.'

'Roger that,' said Valentina.

Roger that? the three other women repeated in surprise.

Valentina blushed. 'It's something Charlie says.'

'Girl,' Sam said, snapping her fingers. 'You got it bad.'

Valentina laughed. 'I know. He's the best.'

'Aha, but is he simply the best?' asked Sam, holding her glass up as if to sing into it again.

'Sam,' warned Zoe. 'More champagne?'

'Okay, okay, I'll save the songs for an "emergency".'

The women sat and Zoe poured them another glass. A happy peace settled over the room.

'Are you sure there isn't more that we can do to help?' Fiona asked. 'I remember when I got married; there was so much to organise. It was so bloody stressful.'

Zoe puffed out her cheeks. 'Since Brad and Barbara took over, there's really nothing to do. In a way, it's a blessing, but I do feel kind of disconnected from it all. Saturday isn't really about me or Rory. The actual ceremony is, and the speeches, too. But the rest of the time we'll be just on display, being dragged about like show ponies to meet randos we'll never see again.'

'You don't have to speak to them,' Valentina said. 'We can establish a perimeter and run interference.'

Sam raised her eyebrows. 'Valentina, I think we need to give you your own call sign. How about "Charlie Sixty-Nine"?'

Valentina laughed. 'Roger that.'

'Seriously, Zoe,' said Fiona. 'Let Brad and Barbara get the photos out of the way, then do your own thing. And anyway, they can't control everything...'

Sam sat up straighter. 'Aha, yes! The hen do!'

'Hen do?' Valentina asked as Zoe groaned.

'It's what we call the Bachelorette party,' replied Sam.

Valentina smirked at Zoe. 'Aha, yes...'

Zoe shook her head, her curls whipping around her face. 'No strippers. No way, no way, no way. The only penis I ever want to see is Rory's.'

'Ah, come on now,' said Fiona. 'You don't have to touch it.'

Zoe scrunched her face as if biting into a lemon.

'I've been married to Dunc forever,' Fiona continued. 'This is my chance to check out a different sausage without actually taking a bite.'

The other women shrieked.

'No,' laughed Zoe. 'Just no.'

'And you're going to wear a sash and an inflatable penis headband,' said Sam.

'Is that when we go to the "make-your-own nipple tassel" workshop?' asked Valentina.

'The what?' Zoe screeched.

'No,' replied Fiona. 'That's for the nude "Paint and Play" party.'

'WHAT?'

'Oh, it's so awesome,' said Sam. 'We get a strip show then decorate the naked men with body paint.'

'In Inverness?' Zoe asked, refusing to believe any of it.

'Well,' Fiona replied with a wink. 'You just need to know where to look...'

THAT EVENING WAS THE REHEARSAL DINNER. IT WAS AN American custom designed to be an intimate and informal evening for the closest members of the bridal party before the wedding, and Zoe felt confident there were enough people present to keep her mother and Barbara from interacting.

However, to help ensure they stayed apart, Clive and his team had laid places at a rectangular dining table in the castle. Rory sat at one end, flanked by his mother and Brad, and Zoe at the other with her parents on either side of her. Between them were settings for Sam and Jamie, Fiona and Duncan, Valentina and Charlie, and Morag and Jim.

Sam, Jamie, Valentina, and Charlie were staying at the castle with Barbara and Brad. They all chatted amiably over drinks with Zoe and Rory in one of the reception rooms as they waited for the other guests to arrive.

Clive entered the room and caught Zoe's eye. She met him by the door.

'Everything okay?' she whispered.

'Your other guests have arrived,' he said under his breath. 'Although, there is a small problem.'

Prickles of panic ran across her skin. 'What kind of problem?'

'Why don't you come with me.'

Zoe followed him through the corridors. She could hear the problem before she saw it.

Her mother and Morag were singing 'Auld Lang Syne' with the tonal accuracy and volume of football supporters, holding each other as they waltzed around the entrance hall.

Fiona was trying unsuccessfully to get them to quieten down, whilst Arnold, Jim, and Duncan stood by looking nervous and uncomfortable.

The women broke apart when they saw Zoe and rushed to embrace her.

'Ma wee darling!' her mother cried.

'Ma daughter from another mother!' Morag joined in.

Zoe checked if the fire extinguisher was to hand as the alcohol fumes hit her.

'Mum! What the hell's going on?' she hissed.

Mary started giggling. 'We, we—' She bent over, snorting with laughter.

Morag tried to hold her up, but her grip slipped and they both tumbled to the floor, Morag farting as she hit the ground.

Arnold and Jim dashed to help as the women's laughter became hysterical.

'What the fuck happened?' Zoe asked Fiona.

Her friend looked to be at the end of her tether. 'They decided to relive their glory days and nick apples from the orchard on the estate. When mum was looking in the shed for a pole long enough to knock them to the ground, she found a load of cider bottles hidden at the back. Fuck knows how long they'd been there for. This is the result.'

Zoe turned to her father. 'Dad! Why didn't you stop this?'

'It's not his fault, Zoe love,' slurred her mother.

'He was out with Jim,' said Fiona, 'trying to get him interested in a hike on the glen.'

'It's not really my cup of tea,' said Jim, glancing apologetically at Arnold. 'It's lovely to look at, I just don't want to be in it.'

'What the fuck am I going to do?' Zoe asked Fiona.

'Zoe!' yelled her mother. 'Watch your bloody language!'

'I've tried to sober them up, but it hasn't worked,' said Fiona. 'Why don't I take them both home, and you can say they've got food poisoning?'

Zoe nodded. 'Yep, good idea. They can't stay here in this state.'

'Oi!' said Morag. 'We're right here, you know.'

'Morag, Mum. You're leaving with Fi. Right now.'

'But it's your funny American dinner thing, darling, we can't let you down.'

Zoe gritted her teeth. Her whole life, Mary had been the quietest and most well-behaved parent she knew. But it seemed her mother's inner party animal had been caged for too long and was now out and on the rampage.

'Mum, I'm sorry, but I can't risk you saying anything to upset Barbara.'

'What? Zoe, she's the one in the wrong. I've been waiting thirty-five years for an apology from her. Do you know what she—'

'Rory!' bellowed Duncan. 'Great to see you!'

Zoe swivelled around. Rory was striding up the corridor towards them, Brad and Barbara by his side.

Zoe stepped forward. 'Unfortunately, Morag and my mother are feeling a little under the weather and won't be joining us this evening.'

'Nonsense!' said Morag. 'We're fine.'

'Doll, what's wrong?' asked Brad.

'Ah, we just ate a couple of apples that were a little off, if you know what I mean,' she replied, winking at him theatrically.

Zoe stared at Rory, seeing her panic reflected back at her.

Brad laughed and winked back at Morag. 'But you're both Scottish, so you can handle it, right, babe?'

'Och, that we can,' she replied. 'Now, Brad, you mustn't get jealous, but I've found myself a fancy-man.'

Zoe could hear Fiona groaning in mortification as Morag pulled Jim forwards. He appeared completely unfazed by meeting Brad.

'Hello, I'm Big Jim. Pleased to meet you.'

Brad looked down at five-foot-six Jim and shook his hand. '*Big* Jim?'

'Aye.' He wiggled his eyebrows. 'I could be known as "*Extremely* Big Jim", but I dinnae want to brag.'

Brad hooted with laughter and clapped him on the back. 'Great to meet you, man!'

Jim grinned and turned to Barbara, giving her a short bow. 'Lady Bauer. May I congratulate you on your marriage. Your husband is a very lucky man.'

Barbara's rigid countenance softened slightly. 'Thank you.'

'Rightie ho, then,' said Morag. 'Let's go and rehearse dinner.'

Zoe sat at the head of the table, relieved there were plenty of people between her mother and Barbara. Jamie may have been sitting opposite Sam but looked as sick as a dog stuck between his mum and Mary. The two women constantly invaded his personal space to talk to each other, whilst occasionally patting him on the head as if he was seven, not twenty-seven. Zoe mouthed a "sorry" at him and he rolled his eyes.

Earlier, as her mother and Morag had stumbled towards the dining room, Zoe had grabbed Clive and told him to water down their wine. So far, the meal had progressed without incident, with both women too drunk and distracted by each other to notice. But Zoe's heart still skipped with anxiety. What might happen now that her mum had left her politeness filters and sobriety back in England?

Clive's team cleared the main course and Mary reached across the table and grabbed Arnold's glass. She lifted it to the light, compared it with hers, and tasted it.

Zoe's stomach turned over. 'Wasn't the beef delicious?' she asked her mother.

'Have you been watering down my wine?' Mary replied before leaning across Jamie. 'Morag, check yours against Big Jim's.'

Oh god.

Morag slurped from Jim's glass, grabbed Duncan's to taste his, then pushed Jamie out of the way to confer with Mary in whispers loud enough to wake a sedated elephant.

'Mine tastes like weak blackcurrant squash compared to theirs.'

Mary took Jamie's half empty glass, downed it, and nodded. 'It's a conspiracy.'

Morag raised her arm. 'Clive!' she trumpeted. 'Can you kindly get me and my esteemed friend here some full fat plonk toot suite, s'il vous plait?'

Clive glanced at Zoe; his face frozen with indecision.

Zoe frantically shook her head at him in response.

Clive cleared his throat. 'I'm afraid we're out of wine.'

'Out of wine?' Morag exclaimed.

The table fell silent.

'But you own a bloody pub!'

Clive pulled the collar of his dress shirt away from his neck, clearly uncomfortable with lying. Zoe's heart thudded faster and faster in her chest.

Clive cleared his throat. 'We've had a delivery issue because of the tree.'

'What tree?' demanded Morag, her eyes narrowing.

'Mum,' said Jamie. 'Shush.'

'Don't you shush me, Jamie ma boy,' she replied.

Jim put his hand on her arm, but she shrugged it off.

'Anyway, there's enough booze in the cellars to sort us out,' Morag continued. 'Isn't that right, Rory?'

Zoe caught Rory's eye and mimed lifting a bag.

He stood.

'There's a good lad,' said Morag.

'I want to thank you all so much for being here,' he began.

'Eh?' said Morag.

Zoe pushed out of her chair and went to his side, holding his hand. He squeezed it as if to reassure her that everything would be okay.

'It means the world to Zoe and me that you have taken this time out of your lives to share this moment with us,' he continued before turning to smile at her. This was the cue for her to continue with the most emotional part of the speech.

She swallowed her anxiety and smiled at everyone. 'We want to give you a gift.'

Surprise murmured around the table.

'Wine?' asked Morag before Fiona hissed at her.

'To thank you for your support, your friendship, and your love,' Zoe continued.

Her mother sniffed. 'I love you, Zoe!' she yelled. 'I love you sooo much!'

Despite how annoyingly drunk her mother was, Zoe grinned back. 'And I love you too, Mum.'

'I love you more!' her mother cried.

Rory took five large bags from Clive and handed them to each of the women at the table.

'Dude,' said Charlie. 'Where's my present?'

'Only one of the presents is specifically for you,' Zoe told him. 'The rest you can share with your better half.'

'If she lets you,' added Rory.

'Aww babe,' said Sam to Zoe. 'You shouldn't have.'

Zoe's chest was full to the brim with love. Both she and Rory wanted to do something personal for the people closest to them, and the fact it was unexpected made the surprise even sweeter.

'So,' Zoe continued. 'The present specific to each of you is a crystal tumbler. It's etched with your name, the date of our wedding, and a map of Kinloch. To go with the glass, you have the choice of a bottle of special edition MacGinley whisky from the GlenWyvis Distillery or a bottle of Scosecco.'

'Sco-what?' asked Sam.

She grinned at her best friend. 'We wanted all the gifts to come from Scotland, so this is the nearest thing to Prosecco we could find.'

'Morag? You ever tried Scosecco?' Mary asked.

Barbara tutted loud enough for the whole table to hear.

Zoe gritted her teeth and forced her smile to stay in place. 'There's also a Scottish silver photo frame for you to put whatever photo you want in it after the wedding,' she continued hurriedly, 'a set of beeswax candles scented with essential oils of Scottish lavender and chamomile, pine, and mint, and a special edition lambswool blanket in the MacGinley tartan.'

'Thank you, both,' said Barbara.

At the other end of the table, Mary was trying to open the

bottle of Scosecco. Arnold tried to assist but she batted him away.

'Twist and tug, Mary,' encouraged Morag. 'Twist and tug. It's just like giving a—'

'Such a thoughtful set of gifts,' Barbara interrupted.

Zoe's head went from side to side as if watching a tennis match being played to the death.

'Give it a shake,' Morag urged.

'I know they will be appreciated for years to come,' Barbara continued.

There was a loud pop as the cork exited the bottle at maximum velocity, along with most of the Scosecco, drenching Arnold and Sam.

'Thar she blows!' yelled Morag, trying to rescue what was left in her empty wine glass.

'The painting!' Barbara cried.

Zoe looked in horror at the wall behind Arnold and Sam. The cork had torn a hole in one of the MacGinley family portraits, right between the eyes.

'Good kill shot, Mary,' murmured Charlie.

'You...' Barbara was white-faced with rage.

Zoe couldn't breathe. It was like watching a car crash unfolding and being unable to stop it.

Brad put his hand on his wife's arm. 'Babe?'

Barbara's chest heaved as she drew in air. 'You're—'

Valentina leapt onto her chair and sang 'Simply the Best' at the top of her voice.

'Ill-bred, ill-mannered—'

Rory started towards his mother as Zoe dashed towards hers.

'Simply the Best!' Sam screeched, standing on her chair and dripping Scosecco as she joined Valentina.

Mary plonked the bottle on the table with a thump. 'At least I'm not a vindictive, stuck-up—'

'Mum!' Zoe cried. 'Stop it!'

Valentina and Sam's singing had now increased in volume to screaming levels.

Mary's face was bright red, her index finger pointed towards Barbara as curses flew from her faster than a witch in a spell-casting competition.

Zoe took one side of her mother, her father the other, and they turned her towards the door.

Glancing over her shoulder, she saw Rory and Brad dragging a shrieking Barbara in the opposite direction.

'Don't worry, Mary!' Morag yelled. 'I'm going to give her a piece of my mind!'

Zoe looked in desperation at Jamie. He was already moving, lifting his mother with Duncan. The two of them strode away from the table with Morag between them, her little legs cycling in thin air as Jim tried to keep up behind them.

They dashed through the castle, Zoe's jaw set tight to hold in her emotions. Marriage was meant to be about the joining of families, but this evening had destroyed any possibility of that. Her mother and Morag were still shouting, but Zoe tuned it out, her heart breaking. This was beyond all her nightmares and she couldn't bear it. There were still three days left before the wedding. How were they going to get through it without another disaster?

4

Thursday – Two days before the wedding – The stag do

Rory frowned at himself in the mirror, a muscle twitching in his jaw.

'Looking good, mate,' said Charlie. 'I'd do you.'

The men were in a bespoke kilt shop in Inverness with Arnold, Jamie, and Duncan for the final fitting of the grooms-men's outfits. It was quiet inside, any sound muffled by the deep pile carpets, the clothing around them, and the bolts of fabric on shelves that reached the ceiling. The front door had been locked and the sign told punters the shop was closed.

Rory wasn't frowning at his outfit; his mind was elsewhere. Zoe's parents had always been a balm to his soul. They were so nice. So bloody normal. Spending time with them was a glimpse into how his childhood might have looked had the stork placed him in another nest. But the animosity between Mary and his mother that had been simmering for the past thirty-five years had now boiled over and he didn't know if the damage could ever be repaired.

His mother had been raging by the time she returned to her old flat in the castle. He knew there was little he could do to talk her down, so he'd left her with Brad and gone to Morag's. There, he found Mary distraught with apologies and Arnold thrusting his wallet at him offering to pay for the painting or anything else broken. That was bad enough, but it wasn't the worst part. That came after he returned to the cabin with Zoe, and she started crying. It had been like a knife in his guts.

'Mate, if you grind your teeth any harder, they'll turn to dust.'

He glanced at his best friend in the mirror. Charlie could read his moods better than he could.

'I know it's not ideal,' Charlie sighed. 'But at least it's happened now, not on Saturday. Remember when Mack got married? The fight in the church before the bloody bride arrived, then two more at the reception? Families are stressful enough. Add in alcohol and a wedding, and you've got yourself a perfect storm.'

'That can't happen again,' Rory said. 'It just fucking can't. But it's impossible for me to be everywhere at once.'

'You don't have to be,' Charlie replied. 'It's my job to deal with shit like this. You don't have to do it on your own.'

His shoulders relaxed a fraction. 'Thanks.'

Charlie slapped him on the back. 'I'm not just a pretty face. And you'll thank me by returning the favour when I marry Valentina in Colombia.'

What? 'You're engaged?'

'Keep it down. No, not yet. I don't want to scare her off. But when it happens, you'll meet her family. Valentina's grannies make your mum look like a pussy cat.'

'May we have the best man?' came the voice of the shop assistant behind them.

Charlie turned. 'That would most definitely be me.' He pulled off his t-shirt and flexed his muscles.

Rory rolled his eyes.

'Good lord!' exclaimed Arnold. 'What a lot of tattoos.'

Charlie kicked off his shoes and stepped out of his trousers.

'Blimey. They're even on your legs.' Rory's future father-in-law stared at Charlie's torso. 'Where does the dragon go?'

Charlie raised an eyebrow.

Arnold took out his phone. 'Can I take a few pictures?'

'Only if you send them to me for my Insta,' Charlie replied.

Arnold nodded. 'Yes, of course.'

Charlie leaned provocatively against a shelf stacked with rolls of tartan fabric. 'Well then, knock yourself out.'

Arnold snapped away.

Charlie hooked his fingers inside the top of his boxers and stared into the middle distance as if trying to work out a complex quadratic equation.

'Do you need to go potty?' asked Duncan.

'Mate,' Rory sighed. 'What the fuck are you doing?'

His best friend struck another pose. 'It's for my brand.'

'Are you selling haemorrhoid cream?'

'I'll have you know,' Charlie replied, 'not only am I going to be the new face of a very famous eau de cologne—'

'*Constipated*, by Calvin Klein?'

'—but I'm intending to be next year's "World's Sexiest Man", and knock Brad down to number two.'

'Speaking of number twos,' Jamie began. 'You sure you don't need to drop the kids off at the pool?'

Charlie grinned, then tugged his boxers lower.

Rory shook his head. 'Mate, really?'

'It's a thirst trap,' Charlie replied, smouldering at the phone.

'A what?'

'A very sexy photo designed to attract attention,' replied Arnold.

Huh?

Charlie raised an arm and flexed his bicep. 'That's right. I quench people's thirst.'

'So, people need to be near death with dehydration before they can face looking at you?' Rory asked, sceptically.

Charlie inclined his head towards Arnold. 'He knows where to find the oasis.'

Arnold promptly turned his back on Charlie to take pictures of Duncan and Jamie. They were dressed in their kilts and pulling their shirts on.

'Arnold, mate, don't waste your skills on them,' Charlie complained.

'If you're thirsty, only a Scot will do,' Duncan replied, pouting at Arnold's phone.

Charlie flipped him the bird.

Jamie tensed his abs. 'Yeah. We're like the finest whisky and you're just cheap beer.'

'Fuck off.'

'That's the ticket, gentlemen,' said Arnold. 'Make love to the camera.'

'Seriously, Arnold? Those muppets?' Charlie asked before pointing at himself. 'Over this?'

Rory threw a kilt at him. 'Put some bloody clothes on.'

'And I mustn't forget the star attraction,' said Arnold, turning his phone to Rory.

Rory froze. His future father-in-law's attention was a little unnerving and reminded him of when Zoe took photos of him for the castle website.

'Arnold,' he asked. 'Why are you taking these?'

'Um... Fun?'

The guilty look that flushed Arnold's cheeks was all too familiar.

Like father, like daughter...

Rory sighed. 'Is this your idea or someone else's?'

His future father-in-law ignored him.

'Arnold?'

Arnold threw his hands in the air. 'Okay, okay, you've got me. Much as I appreciate your excellent physiques, these photos aren't for me. They're for the "thirsty girls".'

'The what?' the men replied simultaneously.

'"The thirsty girls". They've told me to take lots of sexy photos of you and add them to our chat group.'

'Your chat group? Was this Sam's idea?' Jamie asked.

Arnold shook his head.

'I bet it was Valentina,' said Charlie.

'No, it would have been Fi,' said Duncan.

'None of the above,' Arnold replied.

'Zoe,' stated Rory. *Of course,* it was her.

There was an unnerving pause before Arnold replied. 'Yes,' he said, nodding vigorously. 'It was Zoe.'

Rory gave Arnold the look he once used in his army days for the most difficult of interrogations.

'Arnold, who asked you to take these photos?' he asked with deadly calm.

There was a pause as everyone waited for his response.

'Morag,' Arnold finally mumbled.

'My *mum?*' Jamie cried as Duncan yelled 'My *mother-in-law?*'

'Well, she asked me not to photograph the pair of you,' Arnold replied hurriedly. 'She only wanted pictures of Charlie.'

Charlie laughed. 'Suck it, Scotties.'

'It was my wife who wanted photos of Duncan,' Arnold continued.

Duncan punched Jamie on the arm. 'Ha! Sam's the only one who wants you, mate.'

'Fuck off,' Jamie grumbled.

'Oh no, Jamie did get another vote,' said Arnold.

Jamie blanched. 'Please tell me it wasn't Zoe or my sister?'

'No,' Arnold replied. 'It was Mrs McCreedie.'

'Fuck my life,' Jamie muttered as Charlie and Duncan cracked up.

Rory couldn't help but smile, but then a sobering thought crossed his mind.

'Arnold,' he asked. 'How many people are in this chat group?'

Arnold frowned. 'I'm not sure, to be honest. It was eight, but Mrs McCreedie is an admin so she keeps adding more.'

RORY DIDN'T UNDERSTAND THE POINT OF HOLDING A STAG event. He didn't feel the need to party like a condemned man celebrating his last hours of life. Marrying Zoe was not a prison sentence with no chance of parole; it was the start of a new chapter in his life that promised infinite happiness and contentment. Also, due to Zoe's inherent sociability, he knew he'd see more of his friends, not less, in the years to come.

But even though he didn't want a stag do, Charlie had insisted, telling him they hadn't had a night out together in over ten years. Rory didn't drink, wasn't much of a people person, and wouldn't cross the threshold of a strip club. He didn't trust any of his old army friends not to drug and then tie him naked to a lamppost in the centre of Inverness, so none of them was coming.

Charlie had invited Arnold, but he'd declined and now had plans to visit the GlenWyvis Distillery for a private tour with Brad. So, Rory was spending the day and evening with Charlie,

Jamie, and Duncan. He'd told his best friend he didn't mind what they did as long as they were outdoors and at least five miles away from any other human.

After the fitting, they had lunch in Inverness. Later, Charlie drove Arnold out of the city in Rory's truck to hand him off to Brad. Rory had expected to do this, but Charlie was adamant that for the rest of the day he had to do exactly what he was told. So now he was standing with Jamie and Duncan outside the station on Academy Street in central Inverness, waiting for his friend.

He soon wished he wasn't.

The strains of Mendelssohn's *Wedding March* carried over the background noise of traffic and people, but the music was not coming from Rory's truck. Driving far too slowly down the road towards them was his grandfather's Rolls Royce. Charlie was at the wheel with the windows down, wearing a shit-eating grin and a chauffeur's cap.

Rory made a move in the opposite direction. However, he found himself imprisoned in a DuncanJamie sandwich.

Charlie rolled to a halt and got out, the music still blaring.

'Turn it off, you twat,' Rory growled. He hated being the centre of attention, and Charlie was currently blocking the traffic.

Cars started beeping.

'What?' Charlie asked. 'Can't hear you, mate.'

Rory's arms were still locked in place by Jamie and Duncan, so he couldn't stop Charlie from placing a set of pink plastic antlers on his head. A crowd was beginning to gather.

'Let's hear it for the stag!' Charlie yelled, encouraging the onlookers to cheer, before popping the boot of the car.

In the distance, Rory could see a policeman proceeding up the street towards them.

'What the fuck are you doing?' he growled to Charlie.

Charlie started handing packs of beer out to the public.

'Just because you're not drinking doesn't mean other people can't,' he yelled over the music. 'I'm distributing your share.'

No matter what time of day, the promise of free booze was always a winner, and the crowd was growing larger by the second. The boot of the Rolls was large enough to stash a body and several suitcases, and currently contained more beer than an off-licence. Rory pulled to get free of Jamie and Duncan. He could have taken either of them on their own, but with their combined strength he was struggling.

'I'm not going to do a runner,' he told them. 'I want to help so we can leave.'

The cars in the queue behind the Rolls were being abandoned as their owners realised free alcohol was on offer. Rory stuck his head in the boot, grabbing cans and handing them off to Jamie and Duncan as if his life depended on it, hoping the policeman advancing towards them would suddenly be called away to deal with a greater crime.

The sound of the *Wedding March* cut out, but any sense of relief was obliterated when it was replaced by *In da Club* by 50 Cent.

'Ladies!' Charlie yelled. 'Take it away!'

Rory looked up in horror as four women dressed in mini kilts and tartan bikini tops started a dance routine for the crowds.

'Charlie!' he roared. 'What the fuck?'

Charlie ignored him and joined the dancers. They made space, passing him a set of pom poms. He matched their every step and gyration as if he'd spent his life training to be the next Justin Timberlake.

'Let's hear it for our stag!' Charlie shouted. 'Rory MacGinley!'

The crowd cheered.

'I can't hear you!' Charlie continued. 'I said, let's hear it for our—'

'Get your kit off!' screamed a woman.

Charlie winked at her and tugged his t-shirt off, twirling it in the air and shaking his hips.

'And the rest!'

Charlie flicked the top button of his jeans.

The crowd went wild.

'Mate!' Rory yelled. 'Stop! We're going to get arrested.'

Charlie pulled the zip down.

The screams of excitement were almost enough to drown out the sound of a police whistle and approaching sirens. But only just.

AN HOUR LATER, THE ROLLS WAS HEADING OUT OF Inverness and Rory was alternating between wanting to punch his best mate and being grateful he was such a charming fucker. Charlie had switched from Magic Mike to James Bond in an instant, moving the car to the side of the road and helping to get the traffic flowing again. Luckily, PC Killen told them he was in a good mood as he'd just started his shift. They got away with a stern warning and their solemn promise that Inverness would no longer be bothered with anything to do with the wedding.

'Where are we going?' Rory asked for the fourth time.

'At least five miles away from any other human, as instructed,' Charlie replied.

'And how does a street party with dancing girls and free booze fulfil those criteria?'

'That wasn't for your stag do. That was just for me.'

Rory looked over his shoulder. 'Did you know about this?'

Duncan and Jamie looked out the windows, trying to repress their smirks.

'I just hope someone filmed my dancing,' said Charlie. 'Unfortunately, we didn't get to the twerking part.'

Rory shook his head. 'I'd honestly forgotten just how much of a knobhead you are.'

Charlie laughed and slapped him on the back. 'Love you too, mate.'

He pulled off the road, and Rory frowned.

'An airfield? Are we going flying?'

'Fifty per cent of the time,' Charlie replied with a grin. 'The other fifty per cent we'll be falling.'

'Skydiving?'

Charlie nodded.

In the forces, he'd jumped out of more planes than he could count. Some guys hated it, but he didn't. He loved the rush of the freefall and the quiet after the chute was deployed.

'But...' He turned to Jamie and Duncan. 'Are you going to watch?'

Jamie shook his head, and Duncan took a card out of his back pocket and handed it to Rory.

'We both got qualified so we could do it with you.'

Rory was lost for words. They'd done this for him?

'As long as you don't count the pilot, we're five miles from another human, just as promised,' said Charlie. 'Can you now confirm that I am officially the best ever best man?'

Rory smiled. 'The day's not over yet, but this is pretty fucking cool.'

Outside the car, Charlie handed the keys to a man who drove it away.

'He's taking it home,' Charlie explained. 'Our drop site is back near Kinloch. It'll be clearly marked.'

Charlie had given Rory's details to the instructors at the

airfield who'd cross-checked with Rory's former unit about his experience. An instructor took Rory to one side and went through the equipment and procedures with him to reassure themselves he was safe to jump. Then they all kitted up and got in the back of the tiny plane.

When he left the army, just over two years ago, he'd let so much go. But now, flying over the Highlands, adrenaline and memories chased each other through his veins. He grinned at Charlie across the cabin. They'd shared so much together, good and bad. Both were now leading lives outside the army, but their friendship had endured. Jamie and Duncan looked more relaxed than he did when he'd first started jumping. They were good men and he was glad to have met them.

All too soon they were throwing themselves out of the plane, the wind buffeting them as they got into position. Below them, the vastness of the Highlands stretched in all directions. Rory picked out the landmarks, the roads, and Kinloch. An overwhelming rush of love for his home filled him as they hurtled towards it. This was his world. With Zoe at his side, he was where he wanted to be.

About halfway down the loch, in a field that Rory guesstimated was about five miles from the village, stood a large white cross. He knew Charlie would want to land in the very middle so broke formation and dived headfirst towards it.

He drifted after deploying the parachute, and landed first just off the centre of the cross and pulled his chute away. Charlie landed second, right in the middle, then flipped Rory the bird. Jamie and Duncan followed shortly afterwards. Waiting for them was another instructor from the school who took their equipment back with him to the airfield.

'That was incredible,' said Jamie, his eyes alight. 'I can't believe you did that all the time in the army.'

'Well, not all the time,' Rory replied. 'There was a lot of boring stuff too. But I loved this.'

Charlie took fishing equipment out of the back of Rory's truck parked in the field.

'We're exactly five miles from Kinloch,' he said. 'You lot can try and catch some fish, then we'll cook everything I've caught because let's face it, I'm the best at everything.'

Duncan turned to Rory. 'Is he always like this?'

Rory rolled his eyes. 'This is him being modest and reserved.'

Duncan shook his head. 'Jesus wept.'

As the day lengthened, they stood at the loch edge with their rods. Charlie took it in his stride that Duncan was better at catching fish than he was, although he claimed that the fish were discriminating against him as an Englishman.

They lit a fire, the crackling flames and the spitting of the salmon filling the silence. This was exactly what Rory had wanted. A chance to spend time with his friends away from the insanity of everyday life and the wedding preparations. His belly and heart were full. For a stag party, it was perfect.

Charlie's phone rang.

'Mate, really?' Rory asked as Charlie took it out of his pocket.

'It's Valentina,' he replied, then answered the call. 'Hey sweetheart, everything okay?'

There was a short silence, then Charlie glanced up and made eye contact with each of them.

'Okay,' he said into the phone. 'We're on our way.'

5

Thursday – Two days before the wedding – The hen do

Zoe's hen do had started sedately in a local spa. Mary and Morag had ducked out of all activities, claiming that the 'young folk' wouldn't be able to keep up with them. Zoe knew the real reason was that they were both nursing hangovers from hell.

Zoe was happy to let them sleep it off and hang out with Fiona, Sam, and Valentina. She needed a break from her mother and Morag and knew what to expect from her friends, even though they had yet to tell her exactly what they would be doing for the rest of the day.

'But I need to know what we're doing so I can get my head around it,' she complained, as polish was applied to their toenails.

'Surprises are more fun,' Sam replied.

'For who?'

'Us of course,' she giggled.

'Are we seriously going to a nipple tassel workshop?'

Fiona snorted into her glass of Prosecco. 'That may not have been entirely true.'

'Please tell me,' Zoe whined. 'Valentina? Take pity.'

'Okay, okay,' said Sam, rolling her eyes. 'After this, we're having a massage and lunch, then we'll go back to the castle to change. Then a taxi into Inverness for dinner and a cocktail making workshop—'

'Ooh!' Zoe interrupted. 'Yum!'

'Yummy indeed,' Sam continued. 'And that's just the barman. Did you know that he also moonlights as a—'

'You promised no strippers!'

'Yes, I did,' Sam replied. 'But you didn't make the others promise, did you?'

Zoe looked to her right. Valentina shook her head; however, Fiona had a twinkle in her eye that she didn't trust one bit.

'Fi?'

'At some point this evening, a professional stripper will make an appearance and dance for you.'

'No!' shrieked Zoe.

'But,' Fiona continued, her hand on her chest, 'you will love it. Cross my heart and hope to die.'

Could it be Rory?

'It's not Rory,' said Fiona. 'He's busy jumping out of a plane.'

'Say what now?' Zoe squeaked.

Sam shuddered. 'Hun, I know exactly how you feel. I tried to watch Jamie jump in training and nearly shat myself.'

'What? What the fuck?'

'Charlie thought Rory might miss skydiving, so he arranged for them to go this afternoon,' said Valentina. 'Jamie and Duncan have been training, so they can do it too.'

Zoe's heart was racing at a million miles per hour. Her

mouth opened and shut as her brain struggled to choose which one of her thoughts to articulate.

'It's fine, Zo,' said Fiona. 'You know how safety conscious Duncan is. He wouldn't be involved with anything that wasn't one hundred per cent above board.'

Zoe finished her glass of Prosecco in one. She looked at Sam. 'You happy with Jamie doing this?'

Her friend was terrified of heights but still managed to smile. 'I'd rather he didn't, but he really enjoys it so I'm not going to stop him. And anyway, it means we can role play my James Bond fantasies afterwards.'

'Ew,' said Fiona, pulling a face. 'My *brother*, remember?'

Sam put on her Sean Connery voice. 'Hello there, Msh Adamshon. Ish that a mirror in your knickersh? Because I just shore myshelf in them.'

Fiona made retching noises as everyone else laughed.

'So, are we coming home after the cocktail making workshop?' Zoe asked.

The women looked at her as if she'd just suggested they join a nunnery at the end of the night.

'Not on your nellie,' replied Fiona. 'How often do I get to go out and let my hair down? We're going clubbing.'

Zoe glanced anxiously at Valentina and Sam. Valentina was an international movie star, and until recently, Sam starred on the UK's most popular soap. In addition to being household names and faces, neither woman was a shrinking violet.

'Don't worry, Zoe,' said Valentina. 'I promise no one will recognise us.'

'Are you dressing up as a Stormtrooper?'

'Ooh!' said Sam. 'I should have got a Klingon costume! I could have gone as L'Rell.'

'And that would have helped us blend in how, exactly?' Zoe asked.

'You're five foot ten and stunningly beautiful,' replied Sam. 'And laugh almost as loud as me. You'll always stand out. But don't worry. I promise that no one will recognise the third most famous person in Inverness.'

'*Third* most famous?' Fiona asked.

'Well,' replied Sam, conspiratorially. 'I've heard the name "Fiona MacDougall" is written on the walls of most men's toilets. Apparently, if you want a "good time", you should ring her up.'

Fiona threw her head back and laughed. 'I'm not just a "good" time. I'm the best. Just ask Dunc.'

ZOE'S WORRIES ABOUT SAM AND VALENTINA BEING recognised were unfounded, due to the women's skills with hair and make-up. Valentina had brought prosthetics and wigs with her from LA, and after an hour, both women looked completely different. Valentina had a light brown bob and glasses, and Sam had brown contacts and long dark hair. The prosthetics were subtle yet effective, and both women had changed the shape of their noses.

'I'm like a hot Cyrano de Bergerac,' Sam said as she pouted at herself in the mirror.

Valentina looked at herself critically. 'Am I Barbara Streisand or Adam Driver?'

Sam chewed her lip. 'Neither. I think you're Howard Stern.'

Valentina snorted and handed Sam her phone. 'Take some pictures so I can send them to my sister. She's going to love this.'

As the two women messed about, Fiona, who was a hair-dresser, pinned up Zoe's hair.

'It's going to be hot in the club; this will keep you a bit cooler,' she said.

'As will the fact this dress has got less fabric than a handkerchief,' Zoe replied, trying to tug the hem lower.

'Well, you did ask to borrow one of my frocks.' Fiona laughed.

'That's because my entire wardrobe is jeans, jumpers, and wellies.'

'And they're not even sexy wellies.'

Zoe grinned. 'I could wear a bin bag, and I don't think Rory would even notice.'

'True. That man only has eyes for you.'

Zoe sighed. She missed him already. Charlie had texted Valentina earlier with the words 'The Haggis has landed', so she knew he was safe. She could now enjoy her night out, knowing that in a few hours she would be back in his arms in their bed.

Fiona flicked her ear. 'Oi, stop mooning after Thor-squared.' She put a pink crown on Zoe's head. It was ringed with penises. 'The taxi's here. Time to go.'

AN HOUR LATER THEY WERE IN A PRIVATE DINING ROOM IN an Italian restaurant that Fiona had discovered a few months ago, the crown hidden in Zoe's bag.

'The food is so good here,' said Fi. 'The last time we came here with Mum and Jim, Mum ordered every dessert except for the fruit salad.'

Zoe's mouth was watering. 'I don't know how I'm going to eat what I want without exploding out of this dress.'

'Lycra,' Fiona replied. 'That dress is magic.'

'In which case I'm having garlic bread, breadsticks, and tagliatelle carbonara to start, pepperoni pizza for the main, dough balls on the side, and tiramisu.'

'Jesus Christ,' said Sam, clutching her stomach. 'Do you want any more gluten on your gluten?'

'I'm lining my stomach,' Zoe replied, taking a large glug of Prosecco.

'In retrospect?'

Zoe grabbed a breadstick and crunched the end. 'There we go. I've introduced the carbs so the alcohol knows what's coming. It's science.'

'If you say so, Doctor Bullshit,' Sam replied as a waitress entered the room.

'You ready to order?' she asked.

'Yes, thank you, Sam replied in a flawless Scots accent. She looked around the table. 'Zoe? Fi? Deirdre?'

Fiona choked on her drink. 'Deirdre?'

'Yes?' replied Valentina in a perfect Stirlingshire accent. She leaned back and smiled at the waitress. 'Lovely to meet you. I'm Deirdre from Falkirk.'

'Oh, my mum's from Falkirk!' the woman replied excitedly. 'What brings you up here?'

Valentina indicated Sam. 'I'm here to visit my friend, Morag.'

Fiona was now coughing. 'Morag?'

Sam slapped her on the back. 'From Kinloch.'

'Which bit of Falkirk are you from?' the waiter asked Valentina.

Zoe held her breath, however Valentina didn't miss a beat.

'Just north, from Carron.'

'OMG, my mum was from Carronshire! Did you go to Larbert High?'

'Yes!' she replied as if overjoyed to discover their mutual connection to a place Zoe was one hundred per cent sure Valentina had never visited.

'I can't wait to tell Mum! Although you wouldn't have been there at the same time as you're too young.'

Valentina nodded, a disappointed look on her face. 'Probably. I'm only twenty-six.'

Fiona snorted as Valentina lost seven years in one sentence.

'I'd like garlic bread, tagliatelle carbonara to start, pepperoni pizza for the main, dough balls on the side, and tiramisu,' said Zoe quickly.

Valentina mouthed 'Thank you' at her as the waiter was distracted and the conversation moved on.

IT WAS DARK BY THE TIME THEY LEFT THE RESTAURANT, CARB loaded and ready for action. Zoe's cheeks hurt from laughing so much and she'd completely forgotten about the promise of a stripper until they entered a private bar at the back of a club and were introduced to their mixologist, Steve. Wearing an open-necked black shirt with a grey waistcoat over the top, tight black jeans and a killer smile, he was the kind of man who knew exactly the effect he had on most women.

'Ladies,' he said, his voice as smooth as his looks. 'Ready to make some magic?'

'Holy shit,' Valentina murmured, her Falkirk accent slipping away.

Fiona plonked Zoe's penis crown back on her head and pushed her forward.

'Our hen wants Sex on the Beach to start.'

Steve raised an eyebrow as he gave Zoe a blatant once over.

'Have you ever had Creamy Sex on the Beach?'

Zoe's brain froze.

'She definitely hasn't,' said Sam. 'But she does like a Banana Hammock. Can you show her one?'

Steve winked. 'I can do everything.'

'I bet you bloody can,' murmured Fiona.

Steve stared at Zoe as if she were a new cocktail he wanted to try.

'You ready for some action?' he asked, unbuttoning his waistcoat.

'Stop taking your clothes off!' she yelled.

He paused.

'I'm sure your banana is simply marvellous, but I don't want to see it please,' she continued. 'Whatever my friends have paid you to take it all off, I will pay you double to keep it all on.' She fumbled in her bag for her purse.

'Zoe—' Fiona began.

'Do you take cards?' she interrupted, thrusting her wallet at him.

'Zoe! Steve is not the stripper!' said Fiona, pulling Zoe's hand back.

'Oh.' *Oh shit*.

Luckily Steve was grinning. 'I've never taken my clothes off at work before,' he began, 'but there's a first time for everything.'

'No!' yelled Zoe, as Fiona screamed, 'Yes!'

Sam stepped between them. 'Cocktails before cock, ladies. The night is yet young.'

Steve appeared the most disappointed but rallied quickly.

'Right, who's ready to be shaken but not stirred?'

'YES, BUT HOW MUCH *EXACTLY* IS A DASH,' VALENTINA ASKED Steve, ten minutes later.

She was making a Long Island Iced Tea and had carefully lined up all the ingredients along the bar.

'Well,' Steve began. 'It's like a wee splash—'

'It depends on your size,' Zoe interrupted, sloshing vodka

into a cocktail shaker. 'I'm two inches taller than most men, so proportionally I need to add more of everything.'

Steve cleared his throat. 'Actually—'

'It's scientific fact,' Zoe continued, now adding gin. 'I read it somewhere—oh fuck!'

The cocktail shaker had reached max capacity, and alcohol was overflowing.

'Don't worry!' Fiona cried. 'I've got this.'

She reached forward, slurped from the shaker, and lifted it to gulp more of the contents.

'Oi!' Zoe yelled.

Fiona put it down and started coughing. 'Jesus wept!' She thumped herself in the chest. 'That's strong.'

'Would it be twenty millilitres or thirty?' Valentina asked Steve.

'What?' he replied, staring at Zoe as she poured tequila into her shaker.

'A dash,' Valentina replied. 'How many millilitres?'

'Er—'

'Sam—I mean Morag!' Zoe yelled to her friend at the end of the bar. 'Worra you making?'

'Magic,' Sam replied. 'I'm reinventing the wheel.'

'With what?'

'Tomato juice and Bailey's,' Sam replied.

'Jesus Christ,' Steve muttered. 'Er, Morag, that's not a great combination.'

Sam pulled a face. 'Says who? Recipes are merely suggestions. I think this is going to be a huge success.'

'I—' Steve began.

'Have you ever tried it?' Sam asked, her eyes narrowing.

He hesitated.

'Aha!' Sam cried, a look of victory on her face. 'See this?'

She pointed at the drink, then at herself. 'This is geniusism at work.'

Her drink looked like someone had been put through a blender, then decanted into a tumbler. Zoe tried not to gag as her friend downed it in one.

There was a brief pause as everyone stared at Sam.

Her triumphant look faltered to be replaced by one of abject alarm. Without another word, she stepped off the bar stool and ran for the toilets.

Steve sighed and ran his hands through his hair.

'Okay,' said Valentina. 'I'm going to split the difference and go for twenty-five millilitres.'

'Have you got any more vodka?' Fiona asked. 'Zoe and I have run out.'

'Er, yes. What cocktail were you making?' he asked her.

Fiona shrugged. 'Don't know. I'm just here to get shitfaced.'

WITHIN AN HOUR, VALENTINA WAS BUZZED, ZOE WAS properly drunk, and Fiona was off her tits. Sam was the least drunk of them all, mainly due to vomiting up her experimental drinks.

'You shure you okay?' Zoe slurred, squinting into her friend's eyes as she tried to remember if they'd always been brown.

'Yeah, I'm fine. It was a tactical chunder. I just need to catch up with you all.' Sam turned to Steve. 'Please can I have something small and powerful before we leave?'

Steve quickly mixed a drink and presented it to her. He seemed extremely relieved the women were now leaving.

'This is a new drink. Small and powerful, just like you.' He winked. 'I'm calling it the "Sam Adamson".'

Sam did a double take.

'This isn't Sam Adamson,' said Zoe, throwing her arms around her friend. 'This is Morag from Kinloch. She's in her sixties and runs the post office.'

Sam necked the drink. 'What gave it away?' she frowned.

'I was at the ceilidh at the end of filming *Braveheart 2*, your accent slips the drunker you get, and your nose is starting to fall off.'

'Bollocks!' Sam turned to Valentina. 'Deirdre, can you fix my face?'

'Of course, chica,' Valentina replied. 'I mean, och, aye, I can, lassie.'

Steve laughed. 'I know you're Valentina Valverde.'

'¡Mierda!'

'Fuck's sake,' Sam huffed. 'I thought these disguises were foolproof.'

'It's brighter in here, and I'm not as drunk as a punter,' said Steve as Valentina smoothed the edges of Sam's nose. 'You'll be fine in the club. Go have fun.'

THE CLUB WAS EVERYTHING IT NEEDED TO BE. THE LIGHTING was low, the music was loud, and the floor was sticky. Thursday was student's night, so the space was packed with horny young people taking advantage of the cheap drinks and each other. A large group of lads dressed in matching kilts and t-shirts had taken over one corner of the room. Zoe couldn't make out what the t-shirts said, but she doubted it was particularly polite.

Launching herself onto the dancefloor, she could feel how drunk she was. As she spun in circles, the room spun faster. She held Sam's hand for balance.

'You okay?' Sam yelled.

She nodded vigorously then stumbled. Valentina and Fiona caught her before she fell.

'Why don't we do the rest of the scavenger hunt? Valentina shouted.

Fiona was looking at her phone and frowning. 'Yes. I don't know what's happened to the bloody stripper. He should have been here by now.'

Zoe's stomach lurched as her mind was assaulted by the mental image of a strange man waving his willy in her face.

'Fi, please, I don't want a stripper.'

'You'll love this one, I promise,' Fiona laughed, before looking crossly at her phone. 'If he ever bloody turns up that is.'

'There are some men in kilts on the other side of the room,' said Valentina. 'We can get a photo of you with them.'

In the restaurant, Sam had laid out the rules of a special scavenger hunt for Zoe's hen do. By the end of the night, she had to have a photo with a policeman, a doorman, a bald man, a barman, a man in a kilt, and a stripper. So far, she was missing the policeman, a man in a kilt and the stripper. She also had to swap clothes with someone, get a piggy back from a man she didn't know, and have a wee in the men's toilets.

'Amazing idea, Deirdre,' said Sam, taking hold of Zoe's hand. 'Let's do this.'

The group of lads were big and brimming with alcohol induced confidence but went quiet as the four women approached. Zoe and her friends may have been extremely unsteady on their feet, but they were beautiful and had at least a decade more sexual and life experience than the men in front of them.

'Right,' said Sam, taking charge. 'It's my best friend's hen night and—'

Two of the men started taking their clothes off.

'Stop!' yelled Zoe.

'You don't want to see our dicks?' one asked, looking put out.

Valentina and Fiona propped each other up, howling with laughter.

'No!' repeated Zoe.

'We want some photos,' said Sam.

'Of our dicks?' the man asked, hopefully, his hand on his kilt.

Sam huffed. 'No.'

'What's wrong with your nose?' he asked.

'Fuck's sake!' Sam turned away and Valentina rushed to fix her nasal malfunction.

'I need a photo with a man in a kilt,' said Zoe. 'And I need to swap clothes with one of you as well.'

The biggest man stepped forwards, pushing the others back. 'You need the captain for this job.'

'Captain?'

'Of the rugby team. I'm Josh.'

In addition to a kilt, Josh was wearing a massive fake orange moustache and a t-shirt with a cartoon of a cockerel on it. Above the bird was written: 'Be Kind to Animals. Stroke my Cock'.

Zoe looked between him and her, trying to work out how her bodycon dress would fit over his bulk.

'Don't worry,' Fiona yelled. 'It's Lycra.'

The men started chanting. 'Off! Off! Off! Off!'

Josh needed no encouragement, losing his t-shirt and kilt in seconds.

Zoe shrieked and closed her eyes, but not before the image of Josh's meat and two veg was seared into her skull.

'Off! Off! Off! Off!' the men continued, now directing their attention to her.

Zoe needed this done quickly. Josh was now swinging his dick in a circle whilst making helicopter noises. The last thing she wanted was to get kicked out by the bouncers.

Sam, Valentina, and Fiona made a barrier by the wall and she shimmied out of her dress, putting Josh's t-shirt and kilt on. Sam slapped the moustache on her.

Beyonce's 'All the Single Ladies' came on and a cheer went around the club.

Josh, now wearing Zoe's dress, grabbed her hand and pulled her into the middle of the dance floor. Sam had once taught Zoe the moves to the song, and it appeared that Josh also knew them. The crowd moved back as the two of them performed. Zoe was at the top of the rollercoaster. She was wasted but having the time of her life. Nothing could bring her down.

Until Josh started twerking.

The twerking was not so much the issue. What was a far bigger concern was that Zoe's dress was barely covering his backside, and his penis and testicles were now on full display. When the shrieks of laughter alerted Josh to this fact, he pulled the hem to his navel and resumed his helicopter impression.

The crowd went wild.

Two enormous bouncers appeared.

The rest of the rugby team intervened and a fight broke out.

Fiona dragged Zoe away and they watched as the team made a break for it, running for the doors.

'Your dress!' yelled Zoe to Fiona.

'Is okay, is okay,' Fiona replied, swaying from side to side.

But Zoe was fixated on the fact that she needed to get it back. Still dressed in Josh's t-shirt and kilt, his ginger moustache hanging half off, she stumbled after them.

She didn't pay any attention to the cold air of the midnight street nor registered the quiet after the ear-ringing noise of the club. She had the messianic zeal that only the extremely drunk can achieve. The single-minded focus that enables someone barely able to string a sentence together to find a chip shop open at four a.m. on Titan.

She couldn't see the men so took a chance and headed left.

'Zoe! Wait!'

Up ahead was a crowd of people. Had she found them?

'Gimme my dress back!' she yelled as she approached with Fiona, Valentina, and Sam hot on her heels.

The group was a mixed bag. A young woman was sitting in a shop doorway, surrounded by male and female friends who looked far too young to be out on a school night. A small amount of blood was on the floor, and she was having her foot bandaged by a man wearing painter's overalls. A policeman was standing next to them.

'There you bloody are!' Fiona yelled at the men. 'You're late!' She turned to Zoe. 'Finally! The stripper's turned up!'

Zoe looked at the policeman. He was young, fit, and good-looking, but that didn't mean she wanted to see his truncheon.

'My name is PC Killen—' he began.

'And you're going to make a "Killin" tonight with this horny hen!' screamed Sam.

However, Zoe had reached her limit.

'Noooo!' she cried, launching herself at the policeman.

'Zoe! What the fuck are you doing?' yelled Fiona.

Zoe knocked his helmet off and attached herself to him like a limpet. 'I don't want to see your willy! Don't take your clothes off.'

'Off! Off! Off! Off!' chanted Sam.

'My name is PC—' the man cried as he fell to the pavement with Zoe still attached.

'Love truncheon!' cried Sam. 'And Zoe's been a very naughty girl.'

'Zoe! Get off him! That's not the stripper!' Fiona screamed.

But Zoe didn't register anything. She was suddenly on her front, her arms behind her in handcuffs.

'What the fuck are you doing?' screeched Sam, launching herself forward to help her friend. She tripped over Zoe, fell into PC Killen, then backwards to the pavement, holding her prosthetic nose.

'Oi! Magic Mike! You broke my bloody nose off!'

You Can Keep Your Hat On by Tom Jones started playing, and out of the corner of her eye, Zoe saw the man in painter's overalls dancing like a dad with two left feet next to a Bluetooth speaker.

'Derek! Stop!' Fiona cried.

Zoe heard the policeman's voice in her ear. 'I'm arresting you—'

Fiona bent over. 'Fuck! I'm going to be—' she started, before vomiting all over the ground.

6

Friday – One day before the wedding

This was Zoe's second time behind bars at Inverness police station, and she hoped it was her last. Thanks to Barbara, she'd been arrested the previous year for a litany of crimes including attempted murder. Now it was for being drunk and disorderly and assaulting a police officer. Unfortunately, this time she was guilty on all counts.

'Derek is a wallpaper stripper,' Fiona said sadly for what seemed like the millionth time.

She'd also been detained, alongside Sam. The three women now sat, minus their belongings and shoes, in a cell that smelled worse than they did. Valentina had escaped the long arm of the law and had been able to alert their other halves sooner rather than later that the hen night had not ended particularly well.

'He wasn't going to show you his tadger,' Fiona continued.

Despite having emptied the contents of her stomach onto the street and an officer of the law, Fiona seemed most unhappy that her hilarious idea to get a painter and decorator to dance for Zoe hadn't gone according to plan.

Derek was an old friend of Duncan's but had been delayed getting into town. He was further side-tracked when he stopped to help the girl who had fallen and cut herself on broken glass.

'It's okay,' Zoe replied. 'I'm just sorry I lost your dress.'

Fiona puffed out her cheeks. 'I don't want it back. I think a night rubbing up against Josh will have soiled it beyond repair.'

'I can't believe he did an impression of a helicopter with his dick.'

'That's nothing,' yawned Sam. 'You should have seen the key grip on *Elm Tree Lane* at a party. He once decorated his as a minion.'

The three women giggled and then lapsed into a sad silence.

Zoe felt terrible every way possible. Physically, she'd reached the hungover state where instant death seemed preferable to continued life, and emotionally, she was wracked with guilt. Apparently PC Killen had met Rory, Charlie, Jamie, and Duncan earlier when they'd caused a breach of the peace. He'd let them off as he was at the start of his shift and feeling generous. However, at the end of it he wasn't feeling so charitable. At the very best they were spending the night in the cells. At worst? Who knew? They hadn't managed to nap, still too drunk, wired, and worried.

Just after nine in the morning, the cell door opened and a female officer entered. She smiled at them kindly. That was all it took for the three felons to burst into tears.

'I'm so sorry!' wailed Zoe.

'We'll never drink again!' cried Sam.

'My son's got a criminal for a mum!' howled Fiona.

'It's okay,' she said. 'We don't think you're likely to be

repeat offenders, and PC Killen is unharmed. We won't be pressing any charges this time.'

This made the women cry even more.

Ten minutes later their possessions were returned to them and they were escorted into reception, where Rory, Jamie, and Duncan were waiting. The three men rose to their feet as the women shuffled forward.

Jamie opened his arms for Sam, but she leapt back. 'Don't come any closer! I stink!'

He hesitated.

'And I threw up,' added Fiona to Duncan.

Zoe caught Rory looking at her outfit, his brow furrowed.

'And, I, er, swapped my clothes with a rugby player,' she said.

'Ah,' he replied. 'Does he need them back?'

She shook her head. 'I don't think so. He ran away after the fight with the bouncers.'

Rory ran his hand over his face. 'Are you okay?'

She hugged her arms around her. 'Yes, but I desperately need a shower and a sleep.'

He pulled her into his arms and led her out as Sam argued with Jamie about not touching her, and Duncan offered to take Fiona home via the sheep dip at Alasdair's farm.

RORY'S TRUCK WAS BLISSFULLY WARM AND QUIET, AND ZOE felt the stress of the night easing away as they left Inverness behind for the Highlands.

'Did you have a good time yesterday?' she yawned.

He smiled at her. 'Once Charlie stopped being a grade A dickhead, it was amazing.'

She grinned. 'Valentina told us that he spent ages learning that dance routine.'

'I'm now dreading his speech at the wedding tomorrow. He won't tell me what he's going to say, only that it's "short and from the heart".'

'Aww, that sounds lovely.'

Rory raised an eyebrow and Zoe laughed.

'The only card I have left is the threat that if he stitches me up, I'll get my revenge at his wedding.'

'Oh my god! Has he proposed to Valentina?'

'No, he's waiting until he's sure she'll say yes, so don't say anything.'

'I won't.' Zoe yawned again. 'I haven't slept a wink all night. As soon as I'm showered, I'm going straight to bed.'

'You want any company? Your t-shirt is telling me to be kind to animals, so I thought I might pet your puss—'

The sound of Zoe's phone cut through the inside of the truck. She took the call.

'Hey, mum—'

'Your dad's missing!' her mother cried.

Zoe put the phone on speaker so Rory could listen in. 'What do you mean, dad's missing?'

'He went to the distillery with Brad yesterday afternoon and didn't come home last night. He said he might stay over at the castle if they got back really late, but he's still not back and his phone keeps going to voicemail.'

Zoe looked at her watch. 'It's only just gone ten. You know how he is with his phone. He never remembers to charge it and is always leaving it places. I'm sure everything's fine.'

Rory's phone rang. He showed Zoe the screen and the flashing word 'Mum'.

'Mum, can you hang on a second, Barbara's just calling. Don't go anywhere.'

Rory pulled to the side of the road and answered the call, putting it on speakerphone.

'He's gone!' Barbara's shrill voice filled the small space.

'What's happened?' Rory asked.

'Bradley didn't come back from the tour with Arnold yesterday. I can't find him anywhere, and he's not answering any of his phones. I'm—'

'Where's my husband?' Mary cried through Zoe's phone.

'I'm more concerned with what he's done to mine!' screamed Barbara in response.

'Mum!' yelled Rory and Zoe simultaneously.

There was a brief silence, then Rory's phone started buzzing.

'There's another call coming in from the distillery,' he said. 'I'm going to put you on hold, answer it, then come straight back. Don't go anywhere.' He didn't wait for her response and switched calls. 'Rory MacGinley speaking.'

Zoe tried to hear what was being said, but Rory had the phone to his ear, and she had her mother muttering from her phone.

'And this was when?' Rory asked. 'Okay. Can you hold onto everything? I'm on the way back to Kinloch. As soon as I have a plan in place I'll ring you back. Thank you.'

He cut the call and put his mother back on the line.

Zoe's heart was pounding. 'What did they say?'

He ran his hand through his messy hair, tugging on the roots and took a breath before speaking.

'Mum, Mary, that was the distillery. After their tour yesterday, Brad left the car and told the staff he'd be back in the morning to pick it up. He then left with Arnold to walk back to Kinloch.'

'Walk?' repeated Barbara and Mary.

'Yes, and they left their phones at the distillery.'

'What?' Barbara yelled.

'If they'd gone by road,' Rory continued, 'it should have

only taken about four and a half hours, so I can only guess that they went cross country and got lost.'

'I'm calling the police,' said Barbara.

'Mum, wait,' said Rory sharply. 'Do not call them yet. Charlie and I are trained for this. I'm coming straight to the castle now. I'll meet you there.' He turned to Zoe's phone. 'Mary, can you get to the castle in the next fifteen minutes?'

'Yes,' she replied.

'Okay, we're hanging up now. See you shortly.'

He cut the call and eased the truck back onto the road.

'Did the distillery say anything else?' Zoe asked.

Rory sighed. 'Apparently your dad was telling his origin story again, and Brad kept wanging on about being at one with nature. Can you ring Charlie and fill him in?'

She nodded. 'Are they going to be okay?

'Yes. It's not freezing at night yet, and it didn't rain. They'll be fine. I promise.'

ZOE HAD BEEN AWAKE SINCE THE PREVIOUS MORNING. SHE was hungry, hungover, smelled worse than a teenage boy's bedroom, and was due to get married in just over twenty-four hours. Whereas other brides-to-be might be fretting over favours, she was panicking about the whereabouts of her father and the most famous movie star on the planet.

Her father had a notoriously bad sense of direction and could get lost in a supermarket. He was currently missing on the glen with Brad, a man who believed in past lives, pixies, and his own preternatural powers.

Charlie met them at the front door of the castle.

'I've got Jamie and Duncan on board, and they've rung a few mates in mountain rescue. We're meeting here in half an hour with OS maps to plan a strategy.' He looked at Zoe with concern. 'You doing okay?'

She nodded. Knowing that Rory and Charlie were both on the case made her feel much better.

Charlie looked relieved. 'Right, whilst Rory and I are doing the easy bit, I'm afraid you're going to have to take one for the team and deal with your mum and Barbara.'

Zoe's heart sank.

'Valentina's been doing her best,' he continued. 'But it's like trying to charm spitting cobras.' He blanched. 'Shit, sorry, that came out wrong.'

Zoe sighed and rubbed her pounding forehead. 'It's fine, I'll deal with them. Where are they?'

'Drawing room. It's mainly soft furnishings and Valentina's removed the pokers from the fireplace.'

Zoe strode quickly down the main corridor. She couldn't hear any raised voices, but when she entered the room, the atmosphere could have been cut with a knife. Her mother and Barbara stood on either side of the room, glaring at each other. Valentina was between them, and as soon as Zoe arrived, she fled.

Barbara was the ultimate ice queen, but Zoe could see the strain around her eyes. She'd only known Brad a few months, and now they were married. Barbara didn't have enough experience to know if he would be okay, whereas her mother knew from decades of marriage that her husband would likely be fine. Zoe went to her future mother-in-law first and took her hands.

'How are you doing?' she asked.

Barbara's lower lip wobbled.

'I—'

'What about me?' her mother interrupted. 'That's your father out there! Been led astray by—'

'Your husband is the one at fault here!' snapped Barbara, dropping Zoe's hand and pointing at Mary. 'It's not enough that you tried to steal Stuart from me—'

'Woah—' Zoe began.

'And now your husband could have killed Bradley!'

'Are you mad?' Mary shouted.

'Enough!' Zoe roared. 'Both of you.' She pulled two armchairs so they faced each other. 'Sit!'

The women complied.

'Now, listen to me very carefully,' Zoe said. 'I am not spending the next thirty years negotiating this weird, and quite frankly, crazy feud. It ends now.' She turned to her mother, her tone softening. 'Tell me, Mum, honestly, how did you feel when you heard dad was missing.'

There was a long pause as Mary's eyes welled up.

'It was like I was in my twenties again,' she said. 'Seeing Uncle Willie carry him into my mother's house. At the time I thought he was dead. He was so dirty and looked so broken.' She swallowed, and tears fell onto her clasped hands. 'I panicked worrying the same thing would happen again, but this time I would lose him forever, and I would be trapped in some kind of strange past where my mother was still alive and I never escaped Kinloch.'

Zoe let out a breath and turned to Barbara.

'And how did you feel when you realised Brad was missing?'

The fingers of Barbara's right hand were fiddling with the engagement and wedding rings on her left. It was a minute before she spoke.

'It felt like my only true chance at happiness had been snatched from me,' she replied quietly.

Zoe held her breath. Barbara opening up like this occurred at about the same frequency as Haley's comet.

'I loved my first husband and thought a life with him would take me away from my parents and make me happy.' Barbara cleared her throat. 'I was right about only one of those things.'

Zoe waited as she dabbed at the corners of her eyes.

'Meeting Bradley was the most unexpected thing that has ever happened to me,' Barbara continued, her voice so low she was almost whispering. 'I didn't believe I could feel such joy. I don't feel I deserve—'

'Everyone deserves to be happy,' said Mary to Barbara. 'And Brad loves you completely.'

Barbara looked up and held Mary's gaze. 'I'm sorry for my behaviour all those years ago. I was a teenage girl and you were a beautiful woman who Stuart wanted. I didn't know what to do to make him notice me.'

Mary opened her mouth to speak but Barbara continued.

'And I'm sorry for how I have acted this week. I know how passionate Bradley can be, and I have no doubt he roped your husband into this hare-brained scheme.'

'Arnold has been waiting for this opportunity for nearly thirty-five years,' replied Mary with a rueful smile. 'I don't think much persuading was needed.'

Mary reached across the gap and took Barbara's hand.

'I'm sorry, Barbara, for being so badly behaved this week. It is extremely out of character for me. I'm so grateful for all your hard work in bringing this wedding together and for welcoming Zoe into your family despite what you may have thought of me.'

Barbara clasped her other hand around Mary's.

'Your daughter is a wonderful woman and a credit to you and Arnold. I couldn't be happier with my son's choice of wife.'

Zoe had only just been holding it together hearing her

mother and Barbara baring their souls, but with those words, her emotions overran and she started to ugly cry.

'Oh darling, don't cry!' said her mother. 'Your dad will be fine I promise!'

Barbara pressed tissues into her hand. 'Your mother is right, Zoe, dear. I have absolute faith in my son. He will bring them home.'

'It's not that,' Zoe wailed. 'I'm just so happy you made up.'

She pulled both women into a hug. However, neither of them seemed to relish the close contact.

'Darling girl,' her mother began. 'When was the last time you bathed?'

Zoe disengaged, and her mother and Barbara looked at her clothing as if noticing it for the first time.

'Be kind to animals,' her mother read out loud, her brow furrowed in confusion. 'Stroke my—Oh!'

'Please tell me you didn't wear that last night in Inverness?' Barbara asked.

'I didn't start the evening wearing it,' Zoe began.

'Have you even been home?' interrogated her mother.

'My goodness me!' Barbara added. 'Where did you spend the night? Not on the streets?'

Zoe was beginning to wish their détente was over.

'Um, no. In the interest of full disclosure, I spent it in a police station.'

๑๐

THE CASTLE DINING ROOM WAS FULL OF PEOPLE DRESSED IN outdoor clothes. They were clustered around an Ordnance Survey Explorer map on the table.

'We know they set out from the GlenWyvis Distillery here,' Rory said, pointing at the map. 'Around 16:00. They can't have gone south or they would have hit the A834 or A835. There are plenty of farm tracks in the area so I'm assuming they either accidentally went due north, or—' He broke off to check that Zoe wasn't in the room. '—They're injured.'

Jamie entered the room with a sheaf of papers containing pictures of Arnold. He handed them out.

'This is Arnold Maxwell,' said Rory to the room. 'He's mid-sixties and about six feet. Relatively fit. We didn't think any of you needed a photo of Brad Bauer?'

Everyone shook their heads. Despite the seriousness of the situation, he could see the excited glint in the eyes of some of the volunteers. Everyone wanted to be the person who found and rescued the Hollywood star.

Rory turned to the woman next to him. She had the air of someone who could scale Everest single-handedly to bring back a casualty.

'Allison, are your teams all good to go? I want to leave from here with Charlie, and have Duncan and Jamie go to the distillery with Bandit to see if they can retrace their steps.'

She nodded. 'We've got you set up with comms, and we'll cover the north.' She glanced up as more people eager to help entered the room. 'Any extras we can send to Rogie Falls, Castle Leod, and other sites along the south road.' She indicated a man to her left. 'Ryan will stay here and coordinate.'

Rory nodded. 'Okay, let's go. Good luck everyone.'

RORY AND CHARLIE HEADED EAST. THEIR PACKS WERE loaded with communication and rescue equipment as well as food and water, a medical kit, and a specialised stretcher with casualty straps, just in case. It still felt light. In their army days, they'd carried more, and weapons weighed a ton.

Charlie picked at the high vis jacket he was wearing, and the bright rucksack cover. 'I feel like a sitting duck.'

'That's kind of the point, mate,' Rory replied. 'We want them to be able to spot us.'

'I know, I know, I just like the idea of creeping up on them, leaping out, and yelling, "Surprise! You're being rescued!".'

Rory shook his head as he grinned. 'Would it make you feel better if you slapped some mud on your cheeks?'

'Ordinarily, yes. But this face is now worth millions—'

'Of what? Pennies after the financial crash of 1929?'

'You're just jealous you haven't been asked to front a cologne campaign.'

'I'd rather sit on a hot poker. What was the name again? "*Eau de Manwhore*"?'

'Remind me what Zoe used to call you? Wasn't it "mutant hobbit-hobo"?'

'You forgot "yeti".'

Charlie laughed. 'Your missus is amazing.'

Rory smiled. 'I know.'

'So, no last-minute wedding jitters?'

Rory gave him the side eye. 'Jitters? I'm not performing in a school play.'

Charlie shrugged. 'Yeah, but you don't like crowds of people. Or even people to be fair.'

Rory grunted. He saw most of the following day as an exercise to be endured to get the outcome he wanted.

'So, as the best man in every sense,' Charlie continued, 'if you need to talk through any concerns, I'm here.'

'We could just have a fight?'

'It wouldn't be fair on you, mate. And besides, my contract says I'm not allowed to.'

'You're such a dickhead,' Rory laughed as he shook his head.

'Yes, but I'm the *best* dickhead. Don't you forget it.'

THEY HIKED QUICKLY, STOPPING FREQUENTLY TO SHOUT FOR Arnold and Brad. Rory didn't make any presumptions about their survival knowledge. Both were intelligent men, but Arnold lived in suburbia and worked as a bank clerk, and Brad lived in LA and worked in the fantasy land of film.

After a couple of hours, they stopped on a high ridge and surveyed the landscape around them.

'If you had zero common sense and a death wish,' Rory asked Charlie, 'where would you head?'

His friend compared the view in front of them to the map in his hand, then pointed towards a steep gully. 'There.'

Rory nodded. 'Difficult to get into, and if you get injured, almost impossible to get out of.'

They set off, jogging down the glen.

Rory loved exercise like this. He was outside, with someone he trusted with his life, and they had a purpose. The going may have been rough, but both men were trained and still battle-hardened from their years in the service. It took them half an hour to reach the edge of the gully. They couldn't see to the bottom but could hear the sound of running water.

'Arnold, Brad,' Rory yelled, as Charlie wolf-whistled.

There was a whistle in response and a faint cry.

Rory took out his radio and called Allison. 'I think we've found them. I'm sending coordinates, and I'll confirm as soon as we've got eyes on them. It's a gully so we might need an assist if they're injured.'

'Roger that,' Allison replied. 'We'll stand by.'

The men secured their packs, tightening every strap, then scrambled down the steep sides. The rocks were loose, and there weren't many handholds. Small trees had grown up from the cracks. Rory pulled on a few, testing to see how much weight they could take. At the bottom was a rushing stream. It wasn't particularly big, but the water was being forced through a narrow gap creating bubbling froth as it tumbled over and around the boulders.

'Arnold! Brad!' Rory yelled again.

'Rory?' a voice answered.

In the distance, behind a huge rock, they spotted the fingertips of one waving hand.

Thank god.

'Stay put!' he called out. 'We're on our way.'

They picked their way forward, occasionally having to dunk themselves in the icy stream to make progress. When they reached the rock, they clambered to the top and looked down over the other side. There, naked and covered in mud, were Arnold and Brad.

'Dudes!' yelled Brad. 'You found us!' He held out his hand, on which sat what looked like rabbit droppings. 'Want some berries?'

Rory clamped his jaw shut to stop it from falling open. The men had removed their clothes and were attempting to use them for other purposes. Each man had a shirt tied around an ankle with a branch poking out the top. Their trousers had been tied together to create a canopy that was about as effective as spaghetti, and their jackets were lying on the ground. Suspended from a tree were a pair of silk budgie smugglers and a pair of striped boxer shorts.

'What happened?' Rory croaked.

'We got a little lost,' Arnold began.

'No, man, nature needed us,' Brad interrupted. 'She called and we came.'

'And we were a little parched after all the whisky,' Arnold continued.

'So, we dowsed for water,' said Brad over the loud noise of the stream beside him. 'And decided to rappel into the gorge.'

'Rappel?' Charlie asked, incredulously. 'With what?'

'Our pants,' Brad replied.

'Trousers,' Arnold clarified.

Rory could no longer stop his mouth from dropping open. A couple of drunk toddlers had more sense than these two.

'However, unfortunately it didn't work quite as planned,' said Arnold. 'And we took a bit of a tumble. I did my left ankle in and Brad did his right.'

'Two sides of the same coin, man!' said Brad, fist-bumping Arnold.

'So we've been putting our survival skills to the test,' said Arnold. 'Mud to keep the midges away, splints for our injuries—'

'And we've been filtering water to drink!' said Brad with excitement, pointing at the underpants hanging in the tree.

'We're the dream team,' said Arnold.

Rory was positive he was in a nightmare.

'Do you have a phone?' Brad asked.

'Yes,' Rory replied, pulling it out. 'Do you want to ring—'

'Awesome, man! Can you get some pics for Instagram?' He high-fived Arnold. 'Hashtag-taking-on-nature-and-winning!'

7

Saturday – The wedding

Rory knocked tentatively on the door, stood straighter and ran his hands through his hair. This was really happening. It wasn't a dream. Inside was the most important person in his life, in the castle bedroom where their passion had exploded for the first time.

Fiona opened the door and gave him a once over.

'You've scrubbed up well, Rory,' she said with a grin. 'Go on in, we'll leave you alone for a few minutes.'

'You look lovely, Fi.'

She lifted onto her toes and kissed his cheek. 'You're a good man, Rory MacGinley. Don't forget, the tiara's in the safe inside for when you get back from the ceremony. Now go see your beautiful bride before everything kicks off.'

She left the room, and Rory entered, shutting the door behind him.

There, standing by the tall diamond paned window, was Zoe in her wedding dress.

She smiled at him and his heart burst its banks. This was why he wanted to see her for the first time when they were alone. Despite the legalities, pomp, and pageantry of the day, the marriage was about the two of them, and he wanted this moment to be private.

'I love you so much, Zoe,' he said, his voice low. 'You're so beautiful.'

She crossed the room and took his hands.

'And you're the most handsome man in the world,' she replied, her eyes shining. 'Do you like the dress?'

He nodded. 'I think it's perfect. But you could wear a feed sack and I wouldn't notice. All I see is you.' His eyes stung with emotion. 'How did I get so lucky?'

She cradled his jaw and kissed him. 'I could say the same thing.'

There was a sharp knock at the door, and Charlie poked his head in.

'You decent?' he asked with a grin.

'Bit late to ask that now,' Rory replied as his best friend entered the room followed by the bridesmaids.

'Oh my god, don't cry, Zoe!' Sam wailed, 'I've only just done your bloody make-up.'

Charlie threw his hands in the air. 'And look at the state of you!' he said to Rory. 'No tears till after the photos. I'm going to have to lend you my concealer again.'

OUTSIDE THE CATHEDRAL, THE MINISTER WAS WAITING WITH Zoe's parents, his mum, and Brad. The previous day, Arnold and Brad had been carried to the nearest road and transported to Raigmore hospital for a check-up. Thankfully they'd only sprained their ankles and sustained some minor cuts and bruises. Arnold had a pair of crutches from the hospital, but

Brad had managed to source a gold pair with diamante accents.

'That's what I'm talking about!' Brad shouted as Zoe took Rory's hand and exited the car. Putting his weight on one crutch, Brad waved at the official photographer. 'Dude! Get the moment!' He started to hobble forward, but Barbara put her hand on his arm to hold him back.

A sudden thought came to Rory as he looked at everyone present. Could they hold the ceremony here? On the steps?

'Don't even think about it,' Zoe whispered out of the corner of her mouth.

'Think about what?'

'Having the wedding here. I know what you're thinking.'

Fucking hell, his soon-to-be-wife was dangerous. 'Can you hear the creak of the cogs in my head?'

She grinned. 'Something like that. But we can't get married here. Morag and Jim are already inside. Can you imagine the shit we'd be in if Morag missed the ceremony?'

Rory shuddered. 'You're right.'

'Congratulations. You've already mastered the secret to a happy marriage.'

'Huh?'

'Admitting your wife is always right.'

The word 'wife' on her lips sent a bolt of primal lust straight to his cock. He bent his head, hovering his lips above hers.

'I cannot wait till I can call you that,' he murmured.

Zoe's pupils dilated and her nostrils flared. He could feel the hot puffs of air as her breathing quickened. After the disasters of the last couple of days, they hadn't had time for sex. His thickening cock bumped against his sporran. A handful of hours now felt like a lifetime.

'Oi!' Sam yelled. 'You're not married yet and I don't want you ruining your lippy.'

Zoe whimpered as he reluctantly removed his mouth from hers.

'Exactly,' added Charlie, punching Rory's arm. 'Do you need a touch up? I've got manscara and manstick to hand in case of emergencies.'

'Fuck off,' Rory muttered. Whenever he was this close to Zoe, he wished the rest of the world would disappear.

The minister cleared his throat. 'Lord MacGinley, are we ready to proceed?'

He looked at Zoe, and she nodded.

'Yes, we are,' Rory replied.

MARY AND ARNOLD, AND HIS MUM AND BRAD ENTERED THE cathedral first. When they were planning the wedding, Zoe had been clear she was not going to be walked down the aisle by her father.

'I'm not a piece of property to be handed from one man to another,' she'd told him. 'I'm a grown woman making my own decisions.' Luckily, Arnold didn't seem to mind in the slightest and was more concerned with getting his speech right for later.

After the wedding coordinator gave them the nod, Rory walked through the doors, Zoe on his arm, with Charlie and Valentina, Sam and Jamie, and Fiona and Duncan following. The September sun shone through the stained-glass windows, and the organ music filled the cavernous space around them.

This was the moment he'd been waiting for since he fell in love with Zoe, and his chest puffed with pride. Finally the stars had aligned and he was marrying his perfect person. As they proceeded up the aisle, his gaze moved across the crowds. His mind went on a whistlestop tour of his life as he caught people's eyes and relived the memories shared between them.

They reached the altar and the music stopped.

The minister raised his arms. 'Dearly beloved, we are gathered here today, in the sight of God, to celebrate the marriage of Rory MacGinley and Zoe Maxwell.'

'Hell yeah!' yelled Brad.

Rory briefly closed his eyes as he heard his mother hissing at her husband to be quiet. Beside him, Zoe stifled a giggle.

'But before we begin, I must ask if any of you know any just cause or impediment why this marriage should not proceed.'

Rory gritted his teeth.

He heard laughter and glanced to his right to see Charlie staring at the congregation, pointing from his eyes to the crowd, then back again.

The minister cleared his throat. 'Wonderful.'

Charlie's death stare changed to a grin, and he gave Rory an enthusiastic thumbs up.

The minister tapped his microphone to stop the wave of laughter in its tracks. 'Shall we commence?'

THE CEREMONY SEEMED TO PASS IN THE BLINK OF AN EYE. Rory hated being the centre of attention, but today, the whoops and cheers as they were declared 'man and wife' and he kissed his new bride didn't bother him. Soon they were in the back seat of the Rolls Royce with Charlie driving and Valentina riding shotgun.

'Well done mate,' Charlie said over his shoulder. 'Now that the legal bollocks is done, want me to drop you off at the nearest airport so you can fuck right off to the Maldives?'

Rory glanced at Zoe. The thought of avoiding all the

rigmarole at the castle was tempting, but he wasn't sure flying to the tropics was the solution.

Zoe grinned at him, then turned to Charlie. 'I'm a redhead and Rory thinks any weather over twelve degrees is too hot so I think we'll give the Maldives a miss.'

'North Pole?' Charlie asked.

Valentina snorted, which set Zoe off giggling.

'What?' Charlie asked.

'Zoe's visiting Rory's north pole after the reception,' Valentina replied.

'Well, if you ask nicely,' Charlie said to her, 'I'll show you the south one in a bit. It's bigger and better.'

'Bollocks,' Rory grumbled.

'We could get them out during dinner for an objective assessment?' Charlie said.

'No!' chorused Zoe and Valentina.

'It'll be like comparing our speeches,' Charlie continued. 'Yours is tiny and limp, whereas mine is long, meaty, and impressive.'

Rory shook his head. 'Is it too late to sack you and give your job to Jamie instead?'

'Jamie? He can hardly string a sentence together in public,' Charlie retorted.

'Exactly,' Rory replied, then sighed. 'Promise me you won't go full dickhead?'

'When have I ever let you down?'

'Well—'

'Actually, don't answer that,' Charlie interrupted. 'I won't offend anyone, I promise.'

'Charlie, why are your fingers crossed?' Valentina asked.

'Sweetheart! Seriously? Whose team are you on here?' Charlie cried.

'Team Zoe,' Valentina replied with a grin.

Zoe leaned forward, high-fived Valentina, then looked at Charlie.

'Put your foot down, Hamilton,' she said. 'We need to get to the castle before everyone else so we can sort the tiara out and get ready for the receiving line.'

'Yes, Ma'am,' he replied. 'Or should that be "yes, Mrs MacGinley"?'

Zoe squealed with excitement. 'Yes, Mrs MacGinley is correct.'

She sat back next to Rory and kissed his cheek. He turned his head, cupping her face as his lips found hers. She gasped and he deepened the kiss. Her tongue swept into his mouth and his cock jerked impatiently under his kilt. Desire roared through him like an inferno.

'Jesus wept,' Charlie said. 'Can you just wait another ten sodding minutes?'

Zoe broke the kiss, breathing heavily, her eyes flooded with lust.

'Not really,' she replied, her gaze still on Rory, her fingers grazing his leg under the hem of his kilt.

Charlie sped up. 'Well see if you can manage five. But if I run us off the road and we all die in a fireball, I want everyone to know it's all your fault.'

'Deal,' Zoe replied, now nuzzling Rory's neck.

He forced himself to stay still, every muscle in his body straining to reach her as the car ate up the miles back to Kinloch.

As the Rolls glided to a halt in front of the castle, Rory leapt out and ran to Zoe's side of the car. In a moment she was in his arms and he was striding towards the front doors.

'I'll keep the rabble at bay whilst you "help Zoe with her tiara",' Charlie called after him. 'Don't be long. I really don't want to have to come and find you.'

'Thank you!' Zoe called back to him as Rory opened the door and started for the main stairs.

Zoe giggled as he jogged up them. 'We did it,' she said.

'Define "it",' he replied, heading down the corridor.

'We got married.'

He paused outside the bedroom door. 'Pinch me.'

She tweaked the end of his nose. 'Do you believe it yet?'

He smiled. 'Not really. It still feels like a dream.'

He opened the door and placed her gently down. This was where it had all begun. Back then, Zoe was wearing Fiona's wedding dress, and Rory thought she hated him. Now she was wearing her own, and she loved him.

'Shall I get the family jewels out now?' he asked.

It was tradition for the Countess of Kinloch to wear the MacGinley tiara on her wedding day, however the insurance was too great to take it out of the castle so Zoe was wearing it to the reception. Rory wanted to place it on her head himself, so he'd carried the safe up to the room with Charlie the previous day.

She pressed herself against him and lifted the hem of his kilt.

'I'll do it,' she replied, scoring her nails up his solid thighs, and reaching to encircle the hard heat of his cock. 'These are the only family jewels I'm interested in right now.'

'Fuck!' he growled. Her touch was fire, scorching across his skin.

'I do love a kilt,' she replied, her breath fast and uneven. 'But I love what's underneath it more.'

He crushed his mouth to hers with a tortured groan and she opened to him, her tongue clashing with his as if she couldn't get close enough.

Every cell in his body lit up as she tugged and twisted up his length, knowing the exact pressure to drive him wild. With her other hand she grabbed his, pushing it under the skirts of her dress. His desire had been simmering all day and had come to a boil. He needed her now. Nothing else mattered.

Under the silk and the net, his hand found the soft skin of her thighs. It was almost his undoing. He rubbed the wet gusset of her underwear and fell apart, pleasure pulsing through him. He hooked his finger under her panties, pressing it into her wet heat.

She broke the kiss with a cry. 'Oh, god, Rory,' she gasped, dropping her forehead to his shoulder, her body shaking.

He lifted her to the bed and laid her down, trying to control his breathing.

'Do you remember?' he asked, circling her clit.

Her breath was ragged, her expression dazed and confused.

'The first time we kissed,' he continued, his heart pounding. He brought his lips to hers, memories and feelings flashing through him.

She moaned into his mouth and reached again for his cock.

He jerked away. 'Not yet,' he murmured, pulling the bodice of her dress down over her breasts. He sucked a nipple into his mouth with a growl.

'Rory!' Her back arched off the bed. He held her down, his fingers and tongue relentless. He knew exactly how to touch her, how to bring her off with such speed and force it knocked the breath from her body.

She surrendered with a scream as her orgasm hit, bucking and writhing on the bed. But he didn't stop. He kept rubbing the tip of his tongue over the hard nub of her nipple and circling her clit until she stiffened again, his name on her lips.

'Zoe, Zoe, Zoe,' he whispered, kissing her neck.

She reached for his cock, swiping her thumb through the slickness at the tip.

Air hissed in between his clenched teeth.

'Now, Rory.'

She lifted her skirts and spread her legs.

He moved between them, gripping the base of his cock as he stared at her.

'Zoe.' He said her name as if the two syllables contained his entire being and the whole of creation. She was his everything.

She crooked her finger. 'Come on, husband,' she said, beckoning him closer. 'Time to consummate this marriage.'

This was it. They were now married. Love rushed through him as he settled between her legs, his cock nudging her entrance.

'Husband,' she whispered, bucking her hips forward.

A deep and primal need to claim her roared inside him.

'Wife,' he growled, thrusting forward an inch.

'Husband,' she repeated, pulling him deeper.

'Wife,' he groaned, burying himself up to the hilt.

He moved slowly and she squeezed around his cock. Sex with Zoe was always a mind-blowing experience, but now that they were married, everything was deeper and sweeter. Her lips found his, and her tongue licked fire into his mouth.

She wrapped her legs around the back of his and he pumped harder, sensations sparking up his spine with every thrust.

'Yes, Rory, more,' she gasped.

He sank his head into the pillow by her neck, exhaling her name as his hips jerked faster.

'Rory!' she cried, clinging to him, convulsing around him with another climax.

His release coiled tighter and tighter until it snapped, and he let go with a harsh cry, shuddering above her as he fractured into a million pieces of light. Everything was pleasure and everything was her. Once again Zoe had rearranged his universe and turned him inside out.

He shifted his weight from her and slumped on the bed, one arm clasped around her waist.

I love you, I love you, I love you.

'I love you, husband,' she whispered, stroking his hair.

'You too,' he managed, his chest still heaving.

'How are you doing?'

His sporran started singing *I'm a Barbie Girl* by Aqua.

Zoe snorted with laughter. 'What the fuck is that?'

He pulled out his phone and showed her the screen. Charlie. He passed it to her and she answered, putting it on speaker.

'Hello Charlie, how are you?'

'I'm dandy, Mrs MacGinley. Is the haggis with you?'

She giggled. 'All present and correct, just a little tired.'

Charlie sighed. 'Poor lamb. I can only imagine how exhausting it is placing a tiara on your head.'

'Fuck off,' Rory grumbled at the phone.

'It speaks!' Charlie replied. 'Now get downstairs. The receiving line is about to start, and it's missing the most vital pieces.'

'Okay, we're coming.'

'No,' he replied. 'I think that happened about five minutes ago. Stop coming and start moving.'

Rory reached for the phone, cut the call, and let his head slump back on the bed.

'Can't we just stay here?' he asked.

Zoe snorted with laughter. 'Come on, it won't be as bad as you think.'

IT WAS.

Rory stood, a fixed smile on his face, shaking hands with people he barely knew or had never met before. He was positive his mother had squeezed in at least a hundred more guests, and the afterglow from his spectacular orgasm was rapidly fading, to be replaced with grim fortitude.

At least his old army buddies were now at the front of the queue

'Mr Mike Hunt and Miss Fanny Munchin,' a loud voice proclaimed.

'Jez!' a female voice hissed in shock.

Rory sighed. As each person or couple started at the beginning of the line, they were announced by Bentley, an old family friend with a voice so loud and cutting, it could shatter stone.

'I'm actually called Daisy,' the woman said as she shook Rory's hand, her cheeks flushed pink.

Rory smiled at her. 'Nice to meet you, Daisy. And I think Jez's new name suits him better.'

'Yes, it does, doesn't it,' she replied, glaring at her grinning boyfriend.

'Mr Ivor Biggun and Ms Connie Lingus,' Bentley continued.

'Why the fuck did I invite you all?' Rory growled at his friend.

'Rory!' his mother snapped by his side. 'Language!'

Jez grinned. 'Because we make Charlie look good.'

Rory gave a harumph and passed Jez to his mother.

She took his hand. 'Jeremy, I see you haven't changed.'

Rory gritted his teeth and bit back a sigh as Hugh Janus, Ivana Hafsechs, Eric Shun, and Anita Dick were announced. It was almost a relief when the line changed to people he barely remembered.

'The Duke of Somerset, Mr Arthur Foxbrooke, and his two wives; Mrs Vivienne Boucher-Foxbrooke, the Duchess of Somerset, and Mrs Dervla Foxbrooke.'

'Vivi! Brad yelled at the taller of the women.

Rory looked to his right, recognising the famous American actress and model that had married a Duke, and then fallen in love with an Irish single mum and invited her into the marriage. Rory had met them at various weddings and funerals and once when they visited his parent's town house in Edinburgh. The three parents were irrepressibly eccentric, but he remembered their kids being remarkably normal.

'Lord Henry Foxbrooke and Lady Estelle Foxbrooke.'

Yes, it was all coming back to him now. Henry and Estelle were twins and the oldest of the Foxbrooke siblings.

'Mr Connor Foxbrooke, Mr Leo Foxbrooke, Ms Willow Foxbrooke, and Miss Summer Foxbrooke.'

Jesus. How many kids did they have?

'I don't know if you remember me,' Henry said as he shook Rory's hand. He looked awkward as if acknowledging that Rory probably didn't know half of the people at his own wedding.

'I do. From Edinburgh about twenty-odd years ago, then at a few weddings?' Rory replied.

Henry's face relaxed. 'Thank you for the invitation and congratulations. This is quite an event.'

Rory gave a tiny eye roll as if to convey that the amount of fuss was the opposite of what he wanted.

Henry nodded in return.

'Henry! Come on, boy!' His father barked. 'Don't hold up the line. It's champagne time!'

Henry's wince was almost imperceptible as he moved on, but Rory felt it.

BY THE TIME THE LAST GUESTS HAD PASSED ALONG THE receiving line, Rory had almost lost the will to live. They'd been standing there for nearly an hour and a half.

'You doing okay, husband?' Zoe asked, her grin lighting up her face.

His heart soared, and the smile he gave back was one of genuine joy.

'Yes, wife,' he replied. Now that they'd greeted their guests, he wanted to step back from the limelight and spend time with the most important person in his life.

'Well done, everyone,' Barbara said. 'Now for the photos.'

A smartly dressed woman wearing a headset and carrying a clipboard strode towards the line, two photographers and a team of assistants following her.

'We'll start in the great hall,' she said. 'Please follow me.'

RORY DID NOT LIKE HAVING HIS PICTURE TAKEN. AND MOST of all, he disliked crowds of people.

'You can do it,' Zoe whispered. 'Your mum can't freeze time. Eventually this will be over and everyone will bugger off. Tomorrow it will seem like a dream.'

'Dream? It's a fucking nightmare,' he muttered back.

Enough wattage to illuminate the whole of Kinloch had been trained on a raised stage at the end of the great hall where the formal photos were being taken. Rory felt like they were the entertainment for the guests who were happily drinking champagne and eating canapes on the other side of the wall of lights.

His stomach grumbled. Nerves and excitement had taken away his appetite, but now it was back with a vengeance.

Charlie appeared at his side. 'Turn your back on them a sec,' he said.

Rory did. Charlie was holding a plate on which a steak had been cut into chunks. Each piece was skewered with a cocktail stick.

'Remember, we don't eat the wooden bit,' Charlie said. 'Sharpy-sharpy in your tum-tum.'

'Thanks, mate,' Rory grunted. He stuck a chunk in his mouth, took two bites and swallowed.

'Chewy-chewy,' Charlie continued as Rory inhaled more steak. 'Or you might chokey-chokey.'

'Uff off,' Rory replied, his mouth full of food.

'Lord MacGinley? Can you please turn around?' one of the photographers called out.

He swallowed the last chunk of meat, and Charlie dabbed his mouth with a napkin.

'Who's a good boy then?' Charlie said. 'Eating all his din-dins! Now back to smiley-smiley!'

AFTER HALF AN HOUR OF PHOTOS IN THE GREAT HALL, THEY were moved to different locations around the castle. After another twenty minutes, he could see Zoe's smile slipping.

Sam pulled them to the side.

'Do you want any more photos?' she asked.

He waited for Zoe to respond. If she wanted to keep going then he'd suck it up.

She glanced at him. 'I don't think I can handle any more,' she said. 'If that's alright with you?'

His shoulders sagged with relief. 'Are you mistaking me for Charlie?'

She giggled. 'Sorry, I'm just so frazzled I don't know which way's up right now.'

'Okay,' Sam said. 'Food starts in half an hour. Why don't you run off and hide for a bit? I'll sort the photographers out.'

Zoe hugged her. 'Thank you.' She took Rory's hand and led him along the corridor towards the main stairs, ignoring the calls from the wedding coordinator.

Finally he was going to get some peace and quiet with the only reason he was going through this rigmarole.

'Zoe! There you are!'

He bit back a sigh as his mother-in-law rushed towards them.

'My darling girl!' Mary cried, her cheeks pink and the feathers on her fascinator vibrating with excitement. 'How are you doing?'

'I'm a bit knackered to be honest, Mum,' Zoe replied.

'Oh, my love, I'm sure you are.' Mary took Zoe's hand from his. 'Let's find somewhere quiet to sit down before the meal.' She glanced at him. 'Your mother's looking for you. She was in the great hall the last I saw her.'

He tried to keep his features calm, but Zoe could read him like a book.

'Mum—'

'It's okay,' he said. 'You go. I'll see you at dinner.'

Mary put her free hand over her heart. 'Bless you, Rory.'

She led Zoe away, and Rory strode in the opposite direction. Right now, if he couldn't have Zoe, he just wanted silence.

At the end of the corridor was a small, unobtrusive door cut into the panelling. Unless you were looking for it, it was easy to pass by. It led to the servants' stairs and no one ever used it.

He opened the door and passed through.

The light was on inside, and Henry Foxbrooke was sitting on the top step.

Henry stood. 'Sorry. I, er...'

'Wanted a bit of peace and quiet?' Rory replied, shutting the door behind him.

Henry gave a rueful smile. 'Yes. I find events like this a bit much.'

'Try being the groom,' said Rory, leaning back against the wall and running his hands through his hair.

'Didn't you want a wedding this big?' Henry asked.

'Fuck no,' Rory huffed. 'A registry office would have done me. But when you're the earl, apparently that's not good enough.' He paused. Henry was going to become the Duke of Somerset one day. 'You must know what I mean?'

Henry passed a hand over his face. 'Yeah, I do. But I don't want any of it.'

'Your title?'

Henry sighed. 'The title, the estate, my family, the lot.'

'Any particular reason?'

Henry gave Rory a look. 'You've met my parents? All three of them?'

Rory nodded.

'And you must know how my father makes money?'

He shook his head. 'I haven't a clue. I like to pretend most of the world doesn't exist.'

'I wish I could,' Henry replied. 'My dad runs sex parties. Been doing it since before I was born.'

Rory shrugged. 'Honestly, I'd rather have your entire family living in my cabin than have Brad Bauer as a father-in-law. Want to swap?'

Henry smiled. 'He is rather... erm, energetic?'

Rory couldn't help but smile. 'He's a Duracell bunny that's been accidentally hooked up to a nuclear reactor.'

The two men lapsed into silence. Rory remembered how he felt about his family's legacy when he was Henry's age. Henry may be better looking and better dressed than Rory, but he looked as Rory had once felt. Like the weight of familial expectations was bearing down on him.

'I never wanted any of this, either,' Rory said. 'But when my dad died, I was forced to come back. You can't avoid what you were born into forever, but you can make it work for you. You're not your father. Do things your way.'

Henry shrugged. 'It's impossible.'

'Bollocks,' Rory replied good naturedly. 'Look at me. When I first met Zoe, she said I looked like I slept in a hedge and called me a man-bear, yeti, mutant-redneck-hobbit, hobo. Now she's bloody married me. I'm living proof miracles can happen.'

Rory's sporran interrupted the moment by playing *I'm a Barbie Girl*.

He glanced at Henry as he pulled it out. 'It's the so-called "best" man.' He answered the call. 'Yeah?'

'It's time for the most important part of the day,' Charlie said in his ear.

'Dinner?'

'No,' Charlie replied. 'My speech.'

'I'm on my way.' He hung up and turned to Henry. 'Grub's up if you want any?'

Henry smiled. 'Thanks. Sounds good.'

8

Saturday – The wedding breakfast

Zoe was in heaven. Her left hand was in Rory's and her right was delivering chocolate mousse and Prosecco at regular intervals to her mouth. Three orgasms had reduced her stress tenfold, and she was now relaxing with her friends.

Rather than have a long top table, she and Rory sat with Sam, Jamie, Fiona, Duncan, Valentina, and Charlie. Her parents were with Morag, Big Jim, and some distant relations, and Brad and Barbara presided over their own table alongside those lucky enough to sit with the King of Hollywood and his queen.

Rory held her hand, his thumb moving back and forth over her wedding and engagement rings.

She finished her pudding and kissed his cheek. 'I love you, husband,' she whispered in his ear.

He turned, his lips brushing across hers. 'I love you more, wife,' he growled.

She grabbed a clump of his hair and deepened the kiss.

A loud whistle broke them apart.

'Plenty of time for that later,' Charlie said. 'Speeches are coming up.'

Rory stiffened beside her.

Zoe squeezed his hand. 'You really don't have to do this, you know.'

'Yes he does,' Charlie interjected. 'A lot is riding on it.'

'What do you mean?'

Valentina rolled her eyes and opened her mouth to speak.

'He's—'

'Duh-duh-duh-duh-duh-duh-duh-duh-duh-duh.'

A fearsome noise erupted from the speakers set up around the great hall, and Zoe instinctively ducked. It sounded like a helicopter was landing on their heads.

What the fuck?

Rory and Charlie leapt to their feet.

'Duh-duh-duh-duh-nee-nah-nee-nah-duh-duh-duh-duh-nee-nah-nee-nah.'

The helicopter sound was now punctuated by sirens and gunfire.

Rory sat back with a thump. 'Brad,' he said to her, shaking his head.

She glanced over to his table, her heart still racing with adrenaline. Brad had a microphone pressed to his lips and was beatboxing, creating noises that were so realistic she still couldn't believe she wasn't in the middle of a war zone. Despite the brace around his ankle, he'd climbed onto his chair and had his free arm extended as if surfing a wave of sound.

She was now regretting their decision to make him Master of Ceremonies.

'Ladies and gentlemen,' Brad rumbled, his voice vibrating low as the high-pitched sirens and semi-automatic weapons continued, interspersed with the whop-whop-whop from air force Brad. 'The eagle is landing!'

The helicopter sound got louder until Brad made a series of noises that Zoe could only imagine were an aural representation of the helicopter crashing into a zoo during a brass band concert.

'Touch down, baby!'

Beside her, Rory dropped his head.

'We came!' Brad cried, punching the air. 'We saw!' he yelled, striking an uppercut it really didn't deserve. 'Them get married! Let's hear it for my son, Rory, and my new daughter, Zoe!'

Dear god.

Zoe turned away from Brad, hoping she'd accidentally started hallucinating. Fiona and Duncan's shoulders were shaking as they hid their faces in their napkins, whereas Jamie looked as if he'd just walked in on his mum and Big Jim having sex. Rory's eyes were closed, a muscle twitching in his jaw, and Charlie was smirking with unrepressed delight. Only Sam and Valentina, with their acting skills, were able to keep a straight face.

Waiting staff circulated with champagne as everyone clapped.

When the applause died down, Brad continued.

'The journey of a thousand miles begins with a single step, and today, Rory and Zoe have started their love marathon. We're gonna be there for these beautiful kids every step of the way. If they stumble, our arms are there to catch them. If they thirst, they can drink from the fountain of our love. Are you with me?'

Charlie jumped to his feet. 'Yeah! I'm in!'

Rory sighed.

'Whoop!' yelled Brad. 'Is that a "yeah", or a "hell yeah"?'

Rory and Charlie's army buddies were seated at a table at the back of the room. They leapt onto their chairs as their wives and girlfriends sank lower on theirs.

'It's a—' Charlie began.

'Fuck yeah!' all the men on the far table yelled.

'Woohoo!' screamed Brad, causing a head-splitting whine of feedback to screech through the speakers.

Zoe covered her ears.

Barbara snatched the microphone from her husband and walked gracefully over to the table where Zoe's parents were sitting.

'The father of the bride,' she said calmly into the mic, before passing it to Arnold.

Zoe breathed a sigh of relief. The only issue now was her dad's speech and how long it would be.

Charlie ran to the side of the room, returning with a stand on which sat a large digital clock set to 00:00.

'Hello everyone,' Arnold began.

Charlie slapped the top of the clock that started a timer, then covered it with a black cloth.

Zoe's eyes narrowed.

Charlie ignored her, sitting back with a smug smile on his face.

'On behalf of myself and my wife, Mary,' Arnold continued. 'I'd like to thank you all for coming today. I think you'll agree it really is a rather splendid do, and we're very grateful to Brad and Barbara for their kindness and generosity in hosting us all.'

He raised his glass to their table. 'I'd like to make the first toast to my new BFF, Brad the Magnificent, and to Lady Bauer.'

Brad waved his gold crutches at Arnold. 'I love you, man!'

As everyone lifted their glasses, Charlie looked across the table at Rory. 'I love you, man,' he said.

'Fuck off,' Rory replied.

'I next want to speak about my darling daughter,' Arnold continued, looking over at her. 'From the moment Zoe arrived, she brought joy into our lives.'

Emotion welled up inside her. She was so lucky to have the parents she did.

Sam passed her a packet of tissues.

'Many of you won't have met Zoe before today, so I'd like to share some of the highlights of her life,' said Arnold. 'Right from the get-go, she had a full head of curly red hair. Indeed, in the maternity suite, all the world and his wife kept popping by to see our little ginger snap. One of the nurses took a photo and sent it to the local paper. That week Zoe won the "bonny baby" competition, although unfortunately the photo was in black and white so everyone missed the technicolour experience.'

A tiny prickle of anxiety scratched at Zoe's stomach, and she tried to catch her mother's eye. Mary's smile was fixed as she gazed at her husband, but Zoe could see subtle flickers of panic on her face.

'And even in that first week of life, she had a wonderful laugh,' Arnold continued. 'I would tickle her tummy and she would chuckle away for hours.'

'Is this speech going to be long?' Rory murmured in her ear.

'Probably,' she whispered back. 'Is your phone in your sporran? Can you message the wedding coordinator and get them to set the fire alarm off if he hasn't stopped in the next ten minutes?'

'But that would set the automatic sprinklers going all over the castle.'

Charlie shushed them from the other side of the table, and Valentina jabbed him with her elbow.

By now Arnold was recounting Zoe's developmental mile-

stones over her first six months, and people's eyes were beginning to glaze over.

Fifteen minutes in, Arnold had only reached Zoe's first day
at Primary school.

Jez was creeping around the edge of the room towards their
table. He went to Charlie's side and had a whispered conversation. Rory frowned at them, but they ignored him. Charlie
made a note on a piece of paper hidden under a napkin, and
Jez scuttled away.

'What's going on?' Zoe whispered to Valentina.

'It's a bet,' she mouthed back. 'He's being a dickhead.'

Another ten minutes passed, and Arnold was detailing
Zoe's GCSE results.

Zoe eyeballed her mother and circled her hand to try and
get her to stop her dad talking.

'Not yet,' Charlie whispered. 'Hang on a bit.'

'And that was when Zoe decided to do A-level maths, and
we thought accountancy might be a sensible career for her to
pursue,' Arnold continued.

Mary tugged her husband's hand, and he glanced at her. She
hissed something at him.

Charlie leaned forward in his seat.

'Er,' said Arnold. 'I do believe I have gone on rather a bit.
Erm, let me wrap this up by saying how proud I am of our
incredible daughter and by welcoming Rory into our family. He
is a wonderful man and I know he will look after our precious
girl with every fibre of his splendid being.'

Charlie stood, his hand hovering over the cloth covered
clock.

'So, please raise your glasses to the bride and groom. To
Zoe and Rory,' said Arnold.

Charlie whipped the fabric off and stopped the clock with
a triumphant grin. His expression was a contrast to the

relieved looks on everyone's faces as they clapped to celebrate the end of Arnold's speech.

Charlie strode across the room to the table at the back, a top hat in his hand.

Zoe watched as his army friends begrudgingly took notes from their wallets and chucked them into the hat.

'I told you,' Valentina said to Zoe. 'Dickhead.'

'Arnold, my dude!' Brad whooped into the microphone. 'Let's hear it again for my blood brother!'

'Woohoo!' cried Charlie, encouraging the crowds as he made his way back to their table.

Rory ran his hands through his hair.

Zoe leaned in and kissed him. 'You'll be brilliant.'

'And now it's time to hear from the main man,' Brad continued. 'Put your hands together for the Earl of Kinloch, Rory MacGinley!'

Rory slowly got to his feet as if it was a herculean effort just to stand. He waved the offer of the mic away and took a piece of paper from his sporran.

Out of the corner of her eye, Zoe saw Charlie standing with his hand suspended over the clock, a shit-eating grin on his face.

Rory swallowed. 'Thank you, Arnold,' he began.

Charlie started the timer.

'Thank you all for coming,' Rory continued. 'Thank you, Mary, Mum, and—' He cleared his throat. 'Brad. Thank you to the bridesmaids and groomsmen, and most of all, to Zoe for marrying me.'

He sat down. Charlie slapped the top of the clock to stop it at fifteen seconds.

There was a stunned silence.

'A toast!' cried Brad. 'To the woman who was not only

Countess of Kinloch in a past life but is Countess of Kinloch in this one! To Zoe!'

As everyone cheered, Charlie carried the top hat back across the room to collect more money from his friends.

'Well done,' Zoe said to Rory. 'I think you've got at least twenty-five years before you have to do that again.'

'Huh?'

'When Shona grows up and gets married, you'll probably want to do a speech.'

'Shona?'

'Yes,' she grinned, kissing him on the end of his nose. 'Your not-yet-born daughter.'

Rory's mouth fell open.

'You're pregnant?' Sam hissed.

'No!'

'What's that? Fiona asked. 'You're up the duff?'

Rory's face was paler than before he made his speech.

'Chica! Congratulations!' said Valentina, raising her glass.

'Shush!' Zoe whispered. 'I'm not pregnant!'

'Are you sure?' croaked Rory.

She took a large glug of champagne. 'Yes!'

Rory slumped a little lower in his chair and rubbed his forehead. He looked utterly wrung out.

Charlie returned to the table with his winnings and sat down with a satisfied smile on his face.

'Bloody love this wedding,' he said, before glancing around the table. 'What have I missed?'

✴ 9 ✴

Zoe opened her mouth to speak, but Brad interrupted. 'Picture the scene!' he cried. 'The first time I ever met Zoe...' He'd managed to clamber back onto his chair and had one arm outstretched as he gazed off into the middle distance. 'It's a dark and stormy Scottish night. The wind rattles the roof tiles and wolves howl in the glen. The time is just past midnight, and the date, 1352. I am the first Earl of Kinloch, and a stranger is knocking on my castle door. "Who goes there!" I cry. "'Tis I," a female voice—'

The microphone was once again snatched from his hand by Barbara who glided over to Zoe.

'Babe!' Brad called out to his wife. 'I was gonna go through our nine past lives!'

Barbara shot him a look that indicated his tenth one was currently hanging by a thread.

'The bride,' she enunciated into the mic before handing it to Zoe.

As she stood, Sam and Fiona wheeled a large screen closer to her, and Charlie stood next to the timer.

'Thank you, everyone, for coming today,' she began. Nerves jumped and jostled for space in her stomach, but she ignored them. She reached for Rory's hand. 'To reiterate what my husband has said—'

Sam, Fiona, and Valentina started cheering, and the sounds carried around the room in a Mexican wave of whoops, shouts, and stamping of feet.

Zoe looked at Rory. His smile was so big it filled her heart to overflowing.

She gave him a wink then turned back to the room. 'I want to thank Barbara and Brad for enabling us to have such a spectacular wedding, and my incredible parents for showing me what love is every day of my life.'

She risked a glance at her mother and instantly regretted it. Mary was already crying and fanning her face with her hands as if that would stop the outpouring of emotion. Her father wasn't much better, his expression contorting as if attempting to hold back a tide of tears. Morag was looking equally emotional as she threw tissues at them and patted Arnold's shoulder.

'I also want to thank my second mother, Morag,' Zoe continued. 'For always having room in her heart and her home for me.'

'Waaaaaaah!' wailed Morag as her own emotional dam gave way. 'Och, Zoe, I love you!'

Big Jim appeared flustered and grabbed the edge of the tablecloth, passing it to Morag.

She lifted it to her nose and blew loudly, upending four glasses and two bottles of champagne in the process.

'Fuck's sake,' Jamie muttered.

'It's okay,' Morag yelled. 'We've got this! Carry on, lass.'

Zoe grinned even as her eyes filled with happy tears. 'I

want to thank Charlie, Jamie, and Duncan for all the support they've given Rory—'

Charlie stood, pointed to himself and bowed.

'Huevón!' Valentina hissed. 'Sit down!'

'And to Fiona, Sam, and Valentina,' Zoe continued. 'For being the best friends a girl could ever have.'

Charlie led the applause as Zoe held her friends' gazes, the love they had for each other filling the space between them.

She turned to Rory and squeezed his hand. The day had been long and tiring, but it was all worth it for the outcome. She was now married to this incredible man.

She moved the mic away from her face. 'I love you,' she whispered.

'I love you too,' he replied, his eyes shining.

Zoe turned back to the room. 'Most of you don't know how Rory and I met. I'm afraid the first time I laid eyes on his hulking form, I thought he was a bear and threw a week's worth of groceries at him.'

Rory tugged her hand, and she glanced down. His eyebrows were raised as if to ask if she was really going to go there. She nodded, and he sighed and shook his head.

A photo of her cabin appeared on the screen next to her, taken just after she'd moved up to Scotland. The windows were broken and grimy, the roof looked alive, and the front door was completely missing.

'This is the cabin I inherited from my great uncle,' she continued. 'I didn't know at the time, but Rory was desperate to move in himself, so he decided I had to go.'

A shocked murmur ran around the room and Charlie sniggered.

The next photo was taken from inside the cabin, showing thirty Highland cows trying to get in via the front door.

'This was his first attempt,' she said.

Another image appeared, this one of Basil, her super cute and fluffy Dumbo rat, sitting inside a bird's nest on top of a box by her sleeping bag.

'And this was the second,' she continued, as half the room went 'awwww', and the other half cringed.

'However, I was not to be deterred. You see, unfortunately for Rory, I had not only fallen in love with Scotland, but I had also fallen in love with him.'

The next slide was one of the photos she'd taken for the castle website. It showed Rory, shirtless and in a kilt, wielding a broadsword atop a battlement. A chorus of wolf whistles from his army buddies met the ones from Charlie, Duncan, and Jamie.

Rory scowled at them.

Zoe giggled and kissed the top of his head. 'I took these photos to help advertise the castle at a time I thought my love was unrequited.' A photo now appeared of the two of them embracing, Zoe wearing Fiona's wedding dress. 'When Fi took this photo,' she continued, her cheeks heating up as she relived their passionate encounter from a few hours ago, 'I never thought my dreams would come true. But standing here now, I know they have.'

She faced Rory, her eyes blurry. 'I may have once called you a "man-bear, yeti, mutant-redneck-hobbit, hobo", but you're also my champion, my protector, and the love of my life. I love you, Rory MacGinley. Thank you for choosing me.'

He stared at her, his face filled with emotion. She lifted her glass but kept her gaze on him. 'To Rory,' she said, her voice wobbling.

'To Rory!' everyone shouted.

Sam took the microphone from her and Zoe sat on Rory's lap, her lips finding his as his arms held her tightly.

'Ladies and Gentlemen!' Sam cried. 'It's the moment you've all been waiting for. It's time for the speech by the best...'

'Women!' yelled Fiona into another microphone.

Valentina leapt to her feet, whooping and punching the air.

Zoe giggled as Charlie rolled his eyes and started the timer. It appeared he'd lost money on Zoe's speech as he was currently taking notes out of the hat and handing them back to Jez.

'I first met Zoe when we were children,' Fiona began. 'She stayed with her great uncle in his cabin for a few months, and Jamie and I spent all our time with her.'

A picture came on the screen of the three of them standing by the edge of the loch. Zoe's hair was an explosion of frizzy curls, her grin as wide as Fiona's. Jamie was standing to the side, much younger and smaller, his hand down the front of his shorts.

'Fi! Fuck's sake!' Jamie cried as everyone howled with laughter.

'Yes,' said Sam. 'The one on the right is now my boyfriend.'

Another image appeared of the three of them sitting in a tree. The same tree Zoe got stuck in twenty years later.

'The Zoe I knew then,' Fiona continued, 'is exactly the same as the one I know now. Fearless, brave, loyal, and funny.'

Memories flooded her as Fiona recounted their adventures over that endless summer. Lighting fires and cooking marshmallows, camping, swimming, and running wild till late in the night as the summer sun kept shining.

Sam then took up the story. 'I met Zoe in Freshers week at Uni. It was the first time I'd ever met anyone as loud as me, and I knew immediately I'd found someone who would understand me in a way so many others hadn't.'

A picture appeared of Zoe dressed as a tiger and roaring at the camera.

'This was taken at a "Law of the Jungle" party, and I think it sums her up perfectly,' Sam continued. 'Zoe is fiercely loyal and loving, and has always been there for me.'

The next photo was of Sam and Zoe on a beach underneath a palm tree. Sam looked extremely thin, pale, and ill. Zoe's arms were around her as if protecting her from the world. A lump formed in Zoe's throat. She remembered how terribly unwell her friend had been back then.

Sam continued telling stories of their adventures over the years followed by how she felt when Zoe left London for Kinloch.

'When Zoe moved to Scotland, I was desperate for her to come home,' she said. 'I thought she'd be back by Christmas and life could go back to normal.' She smiled at Zoe. 'But life never stands still, and Zoe's bravery in sticking it out in her shed—'

'Cabin!' Zoe yelled, despite the happy tears in her eyes.

'—despite what the weather or Thor-squared threw at her, is a testament to her spirit,' Sam continued. 'And not only did Zoe meet and fall in love with Rory, but thanks to her, my life changed for the better too. Being friends with Zoe is a gift that keeps on giving. When she moved to Scotland, I didn't lose a friend, I gained new ones, a new family, and my own happy-ever-after.'

Sam held up her glass.

'Wait for it,' Fiona said to her.

Sam switched her attention from Zoe to the clock where Charlie's hand was suspended over the switch to stop the count.

Charlie frowned. 'What the—'

'So, ladies and gentlemen, I'd like you to raise your glasses,' Sam said, speaking slowly. 'To the bestest friend anyone could ever hope to have and her very own Prince Charming.'

'To Zoe and Rory!' Fiona and Sam said together as Charlie slapped the top of the clock.

'To Zoe and Rory!' The room echoed as Valentina punched the air and grabbed Charlie's hat of money.

'Fix!' Charlie yelled. 'It's a set-up!'

Valentina pulled his head to hers and whispered something in his ear.

His frown promptly turned upside down.

'Do we want to know what you just said?' Sam asked.

Charlie wiggled his eyebrows. 'Well,' he began. 'Valen—'

Valentina slapped her hand over his mouth. 'Huevón!'

Charlie laughed and kissed her hand before peeling it away.

'You were just saying how much you were looking forward to my speech,' he said. 'Weren't you, sweetheart?'

Valentina smiled. 'Yes, Charlie. That is correct.'

Charlie stood, taking a microphone from Sam. 'Ladies and gentlemen, all that has come before was merely a warm up. An aperitif for the main event and the only reason you're really here.'

People laughed, and there was a chorus of whistles from the table at the back.

Rory sighed, and Zoe whispered in his ear. 'Valentina promised it would be okay. He won't dare cross her.'

Rory harumphed in return.

'Yes, ladies, gentlemen, and the numpties that are Mike, Ivor, Hugh and Eric—'

There were more whistles from his army friends.

'You're all here for the best man, and let's face it, that's me.'

Rory shook his head and flipped Charlie the bird.

Charlie winked back.

'So, let's take you back to when I first met the future Earl of Kinloch, aged eighteen.'

A picture of Rory and Charlie, both sporting buzz cuts and

attempting to appear menacing but looking stupidly young in their army fatigues, flashed up on the screen.

Zoe gasped. 'Your hair!'

'We were young,' Charlie continued. 'We were dumb... We were full of...confidence.'

The screen lit up with more photos of the two of them holding guns, their faces smeared with war paint. Zoe had never seen any of these before. It was like seeing a whole new part of Rory that she'd only ever imagined from his stories.

'We served together for many years, finally achieving our goal of getting our own special forces sunglasses.'

The two men stood in the desert, their arms around each other. The photo had been edited to show black bars across their eyes.

'But it wasn't all fun and games,' Charlie continued, his face sombre. 'We lost many friends and nearly our own lives. I wouldn't be here giving this speech today if not for Rory. He saved my life on more than one occasion and also kept me sane during some dark times. If you know him well, you'll know he's a man of very few words. The most I can normally get out of him are "mate", "fuck off", and "you twat".'

Rory nodded as everyone laughed.

'But when he isn't slagging me off, he's the best friend and comrade a man could ever have. I trust him with my life and would lay down my own for him in a heartbeat.'

Valentina was blinking rapidly as she stared at Charlie, and Zoe felt the lump rise again in her throat.

'When Rory first told me about Zoe,' Charlie continued, 'I thought he was hallucinating. He claimed he'd found his ideal woman in a cabin in the middle of nowhere. But when he told me she called him a mutant hobbit and threw a tin of baked beans at him, I not only knew that she was real but also that she was perfect.'

Charlie held Zoe's gaze. 'Zoe, you're epic. Thank you for making my best mate so ridiculously happy and for enabling me to see more of him than I have in the last few years.'

She nodded at Charlie, too emotional to speak.

'Finally,' Charlie said to the room. 'I want to tell you all a story I've never shared with anyone outside of our unit before. This incident scarred us all for life, and it's very difficult, even now, to talk about it.'

He broke off, bowed his head and pinched the bridge of his nose.

Zoe looked at Rory, raising her eyebrows in question.

He pulled a confused face and shrugged in response.

Everyone was silent as they waited.

Charlie sighed. 'What he did for our unit, that dark night in Afghanistan will stay with us forever. It means more than words.'

An acoustic guitar began to play and Zoe's head shot towards Jamie. He grinned at her and stood next to Charlie, playing the start of 'More than Words' by Extreme.

Rory lowered his head with an audible groan.

'Yes, ladies and gentlemen,' Charlie said over Jamie's playing. 'That night we were introduced to the terrifying sound of Rory singing. Banned by the Geneva Conventions and illegal in eighty-four countries across the globe. His voice can sour milk at a hundred paces and is guaranteed to make your ears bleed.'

Jamie played a little louder and Charlie started singing.

His voice was incredible. He sang as if he'd been brought up in heaven and taught to sing by the angel Gabriel himself.

'Holy shit,' Zoe whispered.

Charlie held out a second microphone to Rory. 'Make it real, mate,' he said. 'Don't tear my heart in two.'

Zoe got off Rory's lap and he stood, like a reluctant mountain. Everyone went wild, cheering and whistling.

He took the mic and stared at her. 'You're married to me now. Please don't ask for an annulment.'

She giggled. 'How bad can it be?'

He gave her a look and took his place next to Charlie.

The room fell silent again, the only sound coming from Jamie's guitar as he played the opening riff.

Rory opened his mouth and began to sing.

Zoe's jaw dropped as everyone at their table apart from Charlie winced. Rory's singing voice wasn't just bad, it was a destroyer of worlds.

If a cat screeched into a microphone whilst running its claws down a blackboard, the sound would still be a soothing lullaby compared to the noises currently coming out of Rory's mouth. It was clear he was trying to find the right notes, but he had the precision of a drunk wrecking ball, and less ability to sustain a pitch than a teenage boy whose voice was breaking.

Charlie attempted to harmonise with him, but the dissonance created a sonic weapon, melting Zoe's brain and making her teeth vibrate. Sam, Fiona, Valentina, and Duncan had their hands over their ears, and Jamie, who couldn't follow suit as he was still playing the guitar, looked green.

The only people who seemed to be enjoying the experience were Charlie and Rory. Charlie had an expression of unbridled joy on his face, and Rory looked as if he'd ceased to give a fuck and was leaning into his own vocal incapability.

Eventually the song finished, and Zoe breathed a sigh of relief.

'Ladies and gentlemen,' Charlie cried. 'If you still possess motor function, let's hear it for the bride and groom!'

After the meal, the tables were cleared and the room was set up for the ceilidh. Now that the formal parts of the day were over, Zoe felt she'd earned the right to kick back and relax with Rory and her friends. For a man who traditionally didn't smile much, her new husband looked as if he wasn't going to stop any time soon.

'Happy?' she asked him.

He pulled her closer into his side. 'Ecstatic,' he replied. 'But please, never ask me to sing again.'

She shuddered. 'I won't. Have I finally found something you're not good at?'

'There's a long list but you're not getting it. I want to keep up the illusion that I'm your perfect man,' he replied.

She reached up and kissed him. 'It's no illusion.'

'Oi!' said Sam, interrupting them. 'Plenty of time for that later. When are you throwing the bouquet?'

The band were tuning up and people were milling around the floor waiting for the dancing to start.

Zoe shrugged. 'Now?'

Sam cracked her knuckles. 'Righty-ho.' She strode into the middle of the room, stuck her fingers in her mouth and whistled.

Everyone fell silent.

'Do we have any single ladies in the house tonight?'

There were a few cheers.

'Any unmarried ladies who wish their man would put a ring on it?'

There was a louder chorus of 'yesses'.

'Okay, then follow me and get your hands up!' Sam cried. 'Because the bride is about to throw her bouquet, and I'm going to be the one to catch it.'

Valentina stalked forward. 'Not if I get there first,' she replied.

'Oh, it's like that, is it?' Sam asked, cocking her hip.

Valentina struck her own pose. 'Hell yes. You're going down.'

The other women who were in the process of joining Sam and Valentina on the floor hesitated.

'Seriously?' Zoe asked. 'Are you all scared of those two?'

There were a few head nods.

Sam cracked her knuckles again and turned to Valentina with a glint in her eye. 'Right then, Valverde. It's just you and me.'

Valentina lifted her chin. 'Bring it.'

'Hang on!' Morag cried. 'Wait for me!'

She thrust her drink into Big Jim's hand and ran towards them.

Zoe looked over at Jamie. His face was pale, and his hand was on his forehead as he watched his mother and girlfriend sizing each other up as if about to fight to the death.

Zoe faced away from them and Charlie began a countdown.

'Three, two, one, throw!'

She launched the bouquet in the air behind her, then turned to see a three-way fight between Morag, Sam, and Valentina as they grappled with the bunch of flowers and each other.

'Jesus Christ,' Rory muttered.

'Go for the eyes and the throat, Valentina!' Charlie yelled. 'You've got this!'

The women were a furious blur of fists and foliage.

Zoe dashed forward. 'Stop!' she screamed.

They did, separating with an equal third of battered flowers each.

'I won!' they all screamed.

Charlie scooped Valentina onto his shoulders.

'The champion, ladies and gentlemen!' he cried, running a victory lap.

'Bollocks!' screamed Sam.

Jamie appeared next to her, and she climbed onto his shoulders.

'Let's hear it for the winner!' Jamie yelled as he set off around the room.

'Jim! Get over here!' Morag cried as Valentina and Sam attempted to continue their fight mounted on their boyfriends' shoulders.

Big Jim had neither the height nor the strength of Charlie or Jamie, and his beloved was heavier than Sam and Valentina combined. He looked nervously at Morag.

Duncan came to his side and said something. Big Jim nodded with relief, and the two of them lifted Morag between them.

'Woo hoo! Make way for the champion!' Morag cheered as she bounced unevenly around the room, a few bedraggled flowers clutched in her fist.

'Bloody hell,' said Rory to Zoe as they watched the carnage unfold. 'I hope I never piss any of them off.'

'Do you think we should start the ceilidh?' she suggested. 'Might help break them up?'

He nodded. 'Good idea.'

She waved at the band and gesticulated for them to begin playing.

The caller grabbed his mic and leapt to the front of the stage.

'Ladies and gentlemen, it's time for the first dance!'

Rory bowed to Zoe and held out his hand. She took it, her heart bursting with happiness as he led her to the centre of the room.

'The happy couple, ladies and gentlemen. Let's hear it for the Earl and Countess of Kinloch!'

'Ha-hang on!' Sam yelled, bouncing on Jamie's shoulders as he ran towards the stage.

Huh?

Jamie set Sam gently down, then took his guitar from a stand.

'Zoe,' Sam said into a microphone. 'I know Rory requested the band play *Never Gonna Give You Up* by Rick Astley for your first dance as man and wife, however I've used my executive veto.'

Jamie started plucking out the opening to *The Heart of Scotland*, the song he'd written with Sam for the film *Braveheart 2*.

Zoe held tighter to Rory, trying not to cry as a wave of emotion rolled through her. This piece of music always spoke to her soul, and now she would forever associate it with the first dance at her wedding.

'Zoe and Rory,' Sam continued. 'This one's for you.'

Zoe turned to face her new husband, looping her arms around his neck. Growing up, she'd never once imagined living in Scotland or marrying someone like Rory. However, life had handed her surprise after surprise since moving north the previous year. Now she felt like a princess who'd found her slightly scruffy Prince Charming.

Sam began singing and everything else fell away. There was no room for thoughts of the past or worries for the future. Her relationship with Rory may have had a rocky start, but they'd built something unshakeable. He recognised and cherished every part of her and was her greatest love.

When the song finished, the room erupted with cheers, applause and stamping feet, but Zoe was hardly aware of any of it. All she saw was the love shining in Rory's eyes.

'Having fun?' Fiona asked her, as she joined them on the dancefloor with Duncan.

Zoe grinned and glanced at her new husband.

'The best,' she replied.

. . .

THE PARTY WENT ON PAST MIDNIGHT, BUT ZOE AND RORY took their leave early. The official line was that they were taking a car to a hotel near the airport and flying out to Barbados the next morning. However, the truth was simpler. They were honeymooning in their own version of heaven; their cabin by the loch.

Rory parked outside, then helped Zoe out of the truck. They stood, hand-in-hand, looking down the gentle slope to the loch. It was dark, but the air still held leftover warmth from the summer. The moon was high, leaving a trail of silver sparkles on the surface of the black water.

The moment was timeless and seemed to hold within it the past, the present, and the future. She was the ten-year-old Zoe who had run wild here with her great uncle. She was the adult Zoe, now married to the Earl of Kinloch. And she was the older Zoe, still holding her husband's hand many years in the future.

'I don't think anything has ever felt so right,' she said quietly.

'I know,' Rory replied. 'It feels like everything that's gone before in my life was just a foreword.' He pulled her closer and kissed the top of her head. 'You're my story.'

She nuzzled his neck. 'With a guaranteed happy ending.'

He swept her into his arms and started for the cabin. 'Just one? I intend on giving you multiple happy endings tonight.'

She giggled as he unlocked the door and carried her inside.

Zoe gasped. 'Oh, Rory!'

Duncan and Fiona had been up earlier to refill the Rayburn stove with wood and check on Basil, but they had also decorated the inside of the cabin with fairy lights and scattered rose petals on the bed.

'Do you like it?' he asked, as he gently set her down.

'Oh my god, this was *your* idea?'

'There's a romantic in me somewhere,' he replied, taking her coat from her shoulders.

She threw her arms around him. 'You're the most romantic man-bear in the whole of the Highlands.'

His smile made her toes tingle.

He brought his mouth to her ear. 'Hear that?' he whispered.

She frowned. 'I can't hear anything.'

'Exactly,' he murmured, moving her hair so he could kiss her neck. 'Isn't it perfect?'

She sighed with contentment. It truly was.

'Happy wedding, husband,' she said, pulling him closer.

'Happy wedding, wife,' he growled before capturing her lips in a blistering kiss.

EPILOGUE

Zoe awoke the next morning, sunlight streaming through the cabin windows.

Rory was boiling a kettle on the Rayburn, still dressed in his kilt and white shirt from the previous night.

'What time is it?' she managed to say, her voice croaky.

He turned and grinned at her. 'Good morning, wife. It's nearly eleven. I don't think I've ever slept that much before.'

'We should get married more often.'

He pulled a face. 'You want to go through all that again?'

She giggled. 'Only the good parts.'

'The tiara fitting?' he asked, pouring a mug of tea. 'Or the wedding night?'

Her cheeks heated. 'Both occasions were pretty spectacular. But your singing was also a highlight.'

He raised his eyebrows. 'Care for a repeat performance?'

She snorted. 'No, ta.'

'Thought not.' He placed the mug on the bedside table and sat beside her, interlacing his fingers with hers and rubbing the pad of his thumb over her wedding and engagement rings.

'Rory,' she began, tentatively.

'Yes, wife?'

She smiled. 'Are you going to call me "wife" from now on?'

He nodded. 'I have to remind myself I'm not dreaming.' He grinned. 'And I do like the idea of bellowing it in public.'

'You're such a caveman.'

'Yep,' he replied, proudly. 'You won't see me hunting broccoli.'

Her smile was so big her cheeks were hurting. She loved him so much.

'Rory?'

'Yes.'

'You don't know what I'm going to ask.'

He shrugged. 'Don't care. I'm fulfilling my husbandly duties. If what you're about to ask for makes you happy then the answer's yes.'

She paused. They'd never really had a proper conversation about this particular subject before. Last night when she'd alluded to it, Rory looked as if he was about to have a heart attack.

'Rory...'

He nodded.

'How do you feel about having a baby?'

He froze for an instant, then scrunched up his face as if in deep thought.

'Has modern science moved along that far?' he asked. 'Does this explain the size of "big" Jim's belly?'

She slapped his arm. 'Rory MacGinley! Don't you ever say that outside of these walls.'

He grinned and mimed zipping his lips shut.

She took his hand and squeezed. 'I've always wanted children, but never met the right person to have them with until you.'

'You really want this?' he asked.

She nodded, suddenly shy.

He stood, ripping off his shirt and throwing it to the floor.

'What are you doing?' she asked.

He unbuckled his kilt and let it drop. His cock was already hard.

'Making a baby and my wife happy at the same time,' he replied, getting on the bed and kissing up the inside of her legs.

'Oh, er, okay, ahh!' she cried as he reached the apex of her thighs.

'Rory,' she gasped.

'Mmmm?' he asked, his tongue flicking over her clit.

Her legs were trembling as each pass fanned the flames of her desire.

'That's not— ah! Um, how you make babies.'

He raised his head, his thumb now drawing circles of fire on the centre of her pleasure.

'It's step one in my process,' he replied. 'Would you like me to stop?'

'No! Don't stop!' She grabbed the back of his head, feeling the vibration of his laughter.

'Don't stop, what?' he asked.

'Please?' she wailed.

'Nope,' he replied. 'Try again.'

'Don't stop, husband?'

'Correct,' he said. 'Now lie back and think of Scotland whilst I fulfil my matrimonial duties.'

Her head flopped back to the pillow, her giggles turning to gasps as his tongue went back to work.

Married life was perfect.

. . .

THE END

❀

Loved Wedding Games?

Don't forget you can read about Rory and Zoe having a baby in Christmas Chaos!
books2read.com/Christmas-Chaos

And want to know more about Henry Foxbrooke? Get Love ad Lib here:
books2read.com/LoveadLib

REVIEW WEDDING GAMES
WRITE A REVIEW & MAKE MY DAY!

Thank you so much for reading Wedding Games! I hope you enjoyed reading it as much as I enjoyed writing it!

Even if just a couple of lines (or a star rating), writing a review is the most amazing thing you can do! It helps people find my books, and lets them know what you loved about them.

You can review Wedding Games at:

Apple

Amazon

Bookbub

Goodreads

Kobo

Barnes & Noble

Google Play

And any other storefront or platform you use!

And, if you want to share more about Wedding Games on social media or your blog, please help yourself to our library of graphics, elements and more via the link below!

www.eviealexanderauthor.com/wedding-games/

Thank you!

Evie

LOVE AD LIB

After all the fun and games in the Scottish Highlands, head to Somerset for the Foxbrooke series!

LOVE AD LIB

Shy and reserved Lord Henry Foxbrooke needs a fake girlfriend. Free-spirited actress Libby Fletcher needs a job. But when they arrive in Somerset for Henry's birthday celebrations, neither are prepared for their reception.

As friendship blurs and faking it starts to feel a little too real, disaster strikes. Can Libby and Henry stick to the script, or has their entire act just bombed?

Tropes

Small Town, Fake Dating, Grumpy/Sunshine, Opposites Attract, One Bed, Different Worlds, Fish-out-of-Water

**Get Love ad Lib now by going to:
books2read.com/LoveadLib**

ACKNOWLEDGMENTS

Wedding Games is dedicated to my husband. All I can say is, he tolerates it.

The second thank you goes to my daughter, who asked me in the summer of 2022 as we paddleboarded down the river Avon, what had happened to this book. Many years ago I had talked about writing Rory and Zoe's wedding but had put the idea permanently on hold. I am very grateful to her for reminding me about the idea and telling me to write it.

My team at Emlin Press: Victoria, Mandy, and Liezl. Thank you for doing everything I can't, won't, or don't have time for. Thank you for tolerating my foul mouth, laughing at my unfunny jokes and sticking around.

Thank you to Aanchal Jain for editing this story and Margaret Amatt, Mike Abolins and Josie Juniper for their additional input. Thank you to Bailey McGinn for designing another wonderful cover and Mark Karasick for taking such fabulous photos of me.

Thank you to my outstandingly supportive friends, in particular my alpha reader, Pash, who has been my biggest cheerleader right from before the very beginning and Margaret (again), who indulges me on a daily basis.

And last, but by no means least, I want to thank my fabulous ARC team, the incredible online community of book lovers and YOU, the reader! Thank you for your continued support and for reading Rory and Zoe's crazy wedding story. Each time you read my books, write me a review and recommend me in countless different ways, my heart gets a little fuller. Thank you!

Evie ♥

Ps - I love love LOVE hearing from my readers so please get in touch via email or social media to ask me anything or just tell me about your day!

NEWSLETTER SIGN-UP

Newsletter freebies are waiting, just for you...

In my newsletter you get Evie news before anyone else, as well as exclusive content and goodies. Newsletter subscribers are my extra special friends, and get everything from bonus epilogues, 19,000 words of deleted sex scenes, free stories, extracts from my current work-in-progress, and exclusive giveaways.

Sign up today!

www.eviealexanderauthor.com/subscribe/

ALSO BY EVIE ALEXANDER

THE KINLOCH SERIES

HIGHLAND GAMES

Zoe's given up everything for a ramshackle cabin in Scotland. She wants a new life, but her scorching hot neighbour wants her out. As their worlds collide, will Rory succeed in destroying her dream? Or has he finally met his match? Let the games begin...

Tropes

Small Town, Enemies-to-Lovers, Grumpy/Sunshine, Fish-out-of-Water, Opposites Attract, Forced Proximity

HOLLYWOOD GAMES

The only way for Rory to save Kinloch castle is to throw open the doors to a Hollywood megastar. However, Brad's plans for *Braveheart 2* involve Rory's girlfriend as well as his home. By saving his estate, is Rory about to lose the love of his life?

Tropes

Small Town, Soulmates, Grumpy/Sunshine, Fish-out-of-Water

KISSING GAMES

Valentina's worked without a break to craft her acting career. But she's never truly lived, and everything's built on a lie. Bodyguard Charlie's done too much living, and is on the run from his demons. Can they let go of the past, or will their love remain a Highland fling?

Tropes

Small Town, Dark Secrets, Bodyguard/Actress, Forced Proximity, Alpha-roll hero, Dating Game

MUSICAL GAMES

After lying to a Hollywood megastar, Sam needs Jamie to write an album with her in just ten days He's got the voice of an angel and the body of a god, but fame is the last thing on his mind. Will he help make her dreams come true?

Tropes

Small Town, Grumpy/Sunshine, Male Virgin, Cinnamon Roll Hero, Opposites Attract, Fish-out-of-Water, Forced Proximity

WEDDING GAMES

Rory and Zoe want to get married. Not easy when their mothers are mortal enemies and Rory's step-father is a Hollywood star with a death wish. Can they unravel the tangles in time to tie the knot, or is eloping the only answer? Get ready for Scotland's wedding of the year!

Tropes

Small Town, Grumpy/Sunshine, Opposites Attract, Soulmates, Fish-out-of-Water

❦

THE FOXBROOKE SERIES

LOVE AD LIB

Shy and reserved Lord Henry Foxbrooke needs a fake girlfriend. Free-spirited actress Libby Fletcher needs a job. But when they arrive in Somerset for Henry's birthday celebrations, neither are prepared for their reception. As friendship blurs and faking it starts to feel a little too real, disaster strikes. Can Libby and Henry stick to the script, or has their entire act just bombed?

Tropes

Small Town, Fake Dating, Grumpy/Sunshine, Opposites Attract, One Bed, Different Worlds, Fish-out-of-Water

AN UNHOLY AFFAIR

Gorgeous Jack Newton has fallen in love with Eveline Shaw. But she's a female vicar dreaming of marriage and kids, and he's a male escort heading out of town. Can Jack show Eveline heaven and keep his secret safe, or are they both headed straight for hell?

Tropes

Small Town, Forbidden Love, Love at First Sight, Sworn off a Relationship, Priest, Different Worlds, Opposites Attract, Dark Secret

THE UPPER CRUSH

Lady Estelle Foxbrooke has lots of names for her dangerously attractive nemesis, James Hunter-Savage, but 'boss' is not one of them. Now, to save her family's estate, she's forced to work closely with him. Too closely.

As the fine line between hate and love starts to blur, sparks fly. Will their relationship ignite and take off, or explode and destroy everything?

Tropes

Small Town, Enemies-to-Lovers, Alpha Hero, Love/Hate, Playboy in Love, Different Worlds, Workplace Romance, Fake Dating

THE LOVE POSITION

Beautiful academic, Sophia Hunter-Savage, has run away to an ashram to reinvent herself. Hot yoga teacher, Isaac Hayward, has left town to avoid the only woman able to tempt him off the spiritual path.

But karma sucks.

Now Isaac's teaching Sophia and they're finding themselves in all kinds of unexpected positions. Will their forbidden love bring inner peace and happiness, or end in a tangled mess?

Tropes

Forbidden Love, Opposites Attract, Teacher/Student, Sworn off a

Relationship, Forced Proximity, Love at First Sight, Different Worlds, Fish-out-of-Water

CHRISTMAS OFF SCRIPT

Ella Chamberlain's in love with her best friend, Leo Foxbrooke. But he's still pining after his first love who left town years ago. Now Ella and Leo are thrown together in the Christmas panto and their on-stage chemistry is starting to appear off it.

Can they find their own happy ending, or are the curtains about to close forever on their friendship?

Tropes

Small Town, Friends-to-Lovers, Best Friend's Ex, Oblivious to Love, Unrequited Love, Fake Relationship

ONE NIGHT ONLY

When Platinum-selling pop-star Avery Taylor's tour is brought crashing down due to an injury, she needs to recover – and fast. But when her nurse turns out to be the devastatingly handsome Connor Foxbrooke, a man she had a one-night stand with a year ago, everything changes. Connor's been burned before and isn't looking for love, but as he helps Avery heal, she starts to mend his heart. Passion blazes, but how can it last when their worlds are so far apart?

Tropes

Second-Chance, Mistaken Identity, One Night Stand, Different Worlds, Opposites Attract, Injury, Forced Proximity, Fish-out-of-Water, Celebrity, Pop Star, Small Town

RIGHTING MR WRONG

Troubled Ronin Tate is on the fast track to self destruction. Sweet-natured Willow Foxbrooke is on a mission to save the world. Thrown together, can Ronin let love in, or will his demons finally destroy both him and any chance of happiness?

Tropes

Emotional scars, Male Virgin, Protector, Opposites Attract, Forced Proximity, Boss/Employee, Different Worlds, Dark Secret, Small Town

UNDER THE INFLUENCER

Sunny Summer Foxbrooke's career as an Influencer is over. Now she's forced to work with grumpy Finn Oakley, the man who's avoided her for years. Will Finn finally return her love, or will she always just be his best friend's little sister?

Tropes

Brother's best friend, Grumpy/Sunshine, Beauty and the Beast, Age Gap, Unrequited Love, Rivals, Different Worlds, All Grown Up, Small Town

By Evie Alexander and Kelly Kay

EVIE & KELLY'S HOLIDAY DISASTERS SERIES

Evie and Kelly's Holiday Disasters are a series of hot and hilarious romantic comedies with interconnected characters, focusing on one holiday and one trope at a time.

CUPID CALAMITY

Featuring **Animal Attraction** & **Stupid Cupid**

Patrick and Sabina have ditched their blind dates for each other. Ben's fighting a crazed chimp for Laurie's love. Insta-love meets insta-disaster in these laugh-out-loud Valentine's day novellas.

COOKOUT CARNAGE

Featuring **Off With a Bang** & **Up in Smoke**

Cute farm boy Jonathan clings to a love ideal, blissfully ignoring what the universe has planned, while keeping track of his pet pig. Posh Brit follows his heart into the American Midwest in search of Sherilyn, his digital dream love.

CHRISTMAS CHAOS

Featuring **No way in a Manger** & **No Crib and No Bed**

In Scotland, Zoe and Rory attempt to have a civilised and respectable rite of passage, but straightforward is not their style. In Sonoma, Bax and Tabi attempt to throw a meaningful Christmas celebration. But there are too many people involved and it's nothing like they expect.

Get all Evie's books at

www.eviealexanderbooks.com

ABOUT THE AUTHOR

Evie Alexander is an award-winning author of sexy romantic comedies with a very British sense of humour.

A self-confessed 'method writer', Evie has taken it upon herself to live a full and messy life, from which romantic and personal failures become fodder for her laugh-out-loud plotlines.

Imaginative, passionate and frequently called 'bonkers' by her friends, Evie's interests include reading, eating, saving the world, and fantasising about people who only exist between the pages of her books.

The first novel in her Kinloch series; Highland Games was released in 2021 and won first place, Best in Category in the The CHATELAINE Book Awards for Romantic Fiction and Women's Fiction 2021 and was a finalist in the American Book Fest awards for Romance Fiction 2022.

Evie lives in the West country of the UK with her family, where she pens her steamy stories from the Smut Hut.

www.eviealexanderauthor.com

- instagram.com/eviealexanderauthor
- facebook.com/eviealexanderauthor
- twitter.com/Evie_author
- bookbub.com/authors/evie-alexander
- amazon.com/Evie-Alexander/e/B08ZJGLP29?ref=sr_ntt_s-rch_lnk_1&qid=1630667484&sr=8-1
- pinterest.com/eviealexanderauthor

Manufactured by Amazon.ca
Bolton, ON